THE PROBLEM WITH LOVE AT FIRST SIGHT

Kammie C. Rose

Hope Avenue Publishing

Copyright © 2022 Kammie C. Rose

All rights reserved

The characters and events portrayed in this book are fictitious. Any similarity to real persons, living or dead, is coincidental and not intended by the author.

No part of this book may be reproduced, or stored in a retrieval system, or transmitted in any form or by any means, electronic, mechanical, photocopying, recording, or otherwise, without express written permission of the publisher.

ISBN-13: 9798847118149
ISBN-10: 1477123456

Cover design by: MiblArt
Library of Congress Control Number: 2018675309
Printed in the United States of America

To those who love to laugh.

CONTENTS

Title Page
Copyright
Dedication
Chapter 1 — 1
Chapter 2 — 8
Chapter 3 — 18
Chapter 4 — 26
Chapter 5 — 33
Chapter 6 — 40
Chapter 7 — 45
Chapter 8 — 53
Chapter 9 — 63
Chapter 10 — 70
Chapter 11 — 79
Chapter 12 — 88
Chapter 13 — 96
Chapter 14 — 103
Chapter 15 — 111
Chapter 16 — 117
Chapter 17 — 128
Chapter 18 — 136

Chapter 19	144
Chapter 20	156
Chapter 21	164
Chapter 22	172
Chapter 23	183
Chapter 24	188
Chapter 25	196
Chapter 26	205
Chapter 27	212
About The Author	215
Books By This Author	217

KAMMIE ROSE

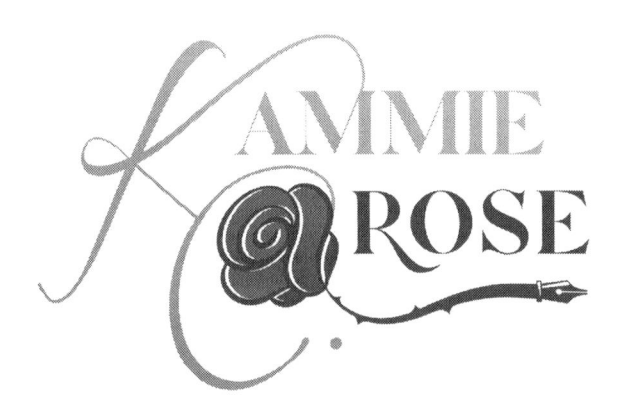

CHAPTER 1

Whatever you might think of me, please know that I'm no bridezilla. Far from it. Go ahead. Roll your eyes. But it's the truth. Yes, my wedding was important to me, but I wasn't obsessed. I just desperately wanted my day to be perfect. That's all. What I didn't know was that everything would devolve into what I would describe as a bride's ultimate nightmare scenario. Something I never saw coming. In fact, no one saw it coming.

Maybe the best place to start this story is on that day at the Santa Barbara Bridal Shoppe.

My wedding dress was ready for its final fitting. I entered the main fitting room wearing the dress for the second time since I bought it. But something was not quite right. Tugging and pulling at the waistline of my wedding dress wasn't helping a bit. How is this possible? The fit was perfect weeks earlier when I first tried it on. My finger wagged at Cassie. "See? This dress feels way too tight." I lashed out at her because she had ignored my strict instructions. "As my maid of honor, your job at the bachelorette party was to slap that plate of appetizers out of my hands."

"I did," Cassie said. "Piper, you're the one who picked them back up off the floor. The blame—and all those calories—are on *you*, girlfriend."

Well, I couldn't blame myself entirely. We *are* talking bacon-wrapped cheese roll-ups here. Still, *I* was the bride. I was vulnerable and finger foods were something a nervous bride is powerless to resist. I like to think of myself as a strong and independent self-made woman—I'm a lawyer for crying out loud. But I was also a bride. And a certain amount of fragility comes with that role. That's why God invented maids of honor. Cassie was supposed to be helping me. What I needed at this moment was for her to take the blame for my recent weight gain. Am I being unreasonable? Being a bride is stressful and that alone should've relieved me of any personal responsibility —especially in the area of emotional snacking. "Cass, you don't need to mention any of this to Jonathan, right?"

Even if the dress was no longer the exact perfect fit, I couldn't maintain my bad mood for long. Standing in the center of the elegant fitting room, my dream was unfolding just as I had imagined. What I was feeling was right out of that movie scene from that iconic rom-com *Pretty Woman*. You know the movie —the one where a super-rich, prematurely graying-haired male hottie meets a woman half his age—after he convinces her, of course, to quit her career as a prostitute, then arrogantly watches as this pencil-thin woman flashes a wide grin with too many teeth and slinks around in that red dress and expensive jewelry and, of course, giggles to the beat of an iconic pop song.

Finally, my life was just like that movie—except for the prostitution, the super-rich older dude, the flashy jewelry, the skinny body, and the surplus teeth. And honestly, the more I thought about it, my life wasn't like that movie at all.

I glanced around the room at the various shapes and sizes of wedding dresses on hangers lining the walls as I stood on a raised fitting platform. All gorgeous dresses for sure, but none of them were as special as mine. I whirled around. "How does the back look?"

After a moment, Cassie said, "It's beautiful."

I spun back to face Cassie. "You hesitated."

"I did not."

"You did. There was a slight hesitation. Okay, what's wrong

with the back?"

"I didn't hesitate."

"There was a pause," I insisted. "There was definitely a pause."

"You asked me to look at the back. It takes a second to study something like that."

"No, it doesn't. Not with a wedding dress. Even if the dress is atrocious, whenever a bride asks someone's opinion, the immediate response should be *it's perfect*."

I made a bee-line for the full-length mirror on the far wall. Until then, I avoided that mirror to check my backside. Every bride these days uses the full-length mirror to see what their dance floor twerking will look like in the dress. There will be no bridal twerking at a wedding where Jonathan is the groom. He might faint. Hey, I'm an educated professional and swore off ever attempting that vulgar, ass-gyrating dance. Especially since the day I witnessed my mother's debut twerk at Cousin Cosmo's wedding. The sight of her moving her body like that—well, I'm still not over it.

Cassie must have figured out she'd better gush over my wedding dress. From the fitting room's plush loveseat, she said, "It's tasteful and so classy. Not overdone like that Bo Peep dress you considered."

She had to mock something—that's her nature—so she ridiculed a dress I almost chose earlier.

"Hey. I liked the big hooky-crook thing. Keeps the groom from running away."

"When he sees you in *this* dress, he won't be running anywhere."

"My mother will think I *sold out*, but I think it strikes a perfect balance. It's traditional, yet will work perfectly at my beach wedding."

"Sold out?"

Turning toward Cassie, I rolled my eyes. "It's too white, she'll say. Then she'll insist I make a bold statement by flaunting a brightly colored wedding dress as some kind of proud indicator that I've already lost my virginity."

"Your virginity? You're twenty-eight."

"What does age have to do with it?"

"Nothing. But when the dress is white and you're twenty-eight, some might wonder. That's all."

"Well, that subject is nobody's business. And all brides wear white, regardless of age or anything else."

Cassie shook her head. "Why isn't the *groom* pressured to wear white? Why doesn't he have to confirm *his* chastity?"

"You're right. Men can show up in a black suit and no one second-guesses that. Although my mother would insist the groom's black suit *is* an indicator."

Cassie smirked. "She's got men all wrong. Every groom dresses like they're going to a funeral. It's all Freudian."

"All I know is the color of my wedding dress is none of my mother's concern. Still, why do I keep worrying about pleasing my avant-garde mother? She and I are two different people."

"Your mother definitely marches to the beat of a different drummer."

"And knowing her, she probably slept with that drummer too." I pressed on both temples with my fingers and exhaled. "I'm trying to walk the line between my wild mother and my traditionalist fiancé."

"Careful. Walking that line might turn into walking the plank."

I laughed. "Believe me; sharks might be easier to deal with."

According to my mother, marriage is not something a proud, independent woman should strive for. And she attempted to drill that mindset into me early on. As sometimes happens with a parent's best-laid plan, this attempt to turn me sour on marriage had the opposite effect. I became obsessed with breaking my female ancestors' multi-generational trend of never marrying. That's why I mentioned earlier that I'm not obsessed so much with the wedding day as I am with being married. I couldn't allow anything to prevent me from reaching my goal. So I kept my eye out for someone to grow old with. He had to be intelligent, grounded, commonsensical, loving,

CHAPTER 1

spiritual, funny, and hot looking. Intelligence was usually my top priority, but sometimes looks would take precedence depending on the day's proximity to the weekend. Regardless of the order, all seven qualities needed to be present.

"Well, no matter what your mother might think of the shade of white, I think you look beautiful. You've got to be the most beautiful attorney ever to wear a wedding dress."

The bridal stylist re-entered the fitting room. She grabbed the eyeglasses hanging from a chain around her neck and placed them on her upturned nose. She asked, "Piper, don't you agree our seamstress is the best?"

"She may need to let it out again," I said.

The bridal stylist tugged the back of the dress with her fingers and said, "It doesn't feel too tight to me." She turned to Cassie. "The other three bridesmaids have already been here and tried on their dresses. Are you ready to try on yours?"

Cassie frowned. "Not really."

I dismissed Cassie's reluctance with a wave of my hand. "She's kidding. She wants to see how it fits."

The bridal stylist smiled. "You'll love it. It's in our stockroom. I'll be right back."

After the stylist exited the room, Cassie groaned. "I'm so dreading this."

I needed to bolster Cassie's confidence. "C'mon, you'll be the most beautiful maid of honor ever."

"No, I won't. I should have known not to let a woman like you—with your amazing body—pick out the style of bridesmaid dresses. I'll be forever captured in photos as that overweight bridesmaid in the dress that's all wrong for her." She furrowed her brow and asked, "A silk mermaid-style dress? Really, Piper?"

"You'll look stunning. Trust me."

"The wedding's on the beach. I'll be waddling across the sand in that tight dress, looking nothing like a mermaid, but more like the cargo ship that *struck* the mermaid." Cassie sighed. "Letting you pick my dress had disaster written all over it."

"You'll look amazing. You'll see." I responded in my best, most positive tone, knowing full well I might be mistaken about how amazing she would look in a silk mermaid dress.

If Cassie ever attempted to wear Taylor Swift's onstage outfit, I would nod my approval—no one else would, but I would. That was our unspoken pact. We protected each other's feelings from the day we became best friends at college. We always looked after each other and had each other's best interest at heart.

Cassie recently took it upon herself to provide me with what she considered an invaluable service—she rated all the men in my life over the last decade. Not just the guys in consideration as serious marital material, but *all* the men, from the casual dates to even my neighborhood postal worker. Though I never dated him, sometimes the mailman scored higher than half the field.

Cassie initiated the rating system with numbers ranging from one to ten, but there were eleven distinct levels, including zero, which she occasionally had to consider. But then she concluded that the nuances from one number to another were too gray, so she switched to a letter grade system. Though she missed the fun of giving some of my dates a zero, an F- was almost equally satisfying, so she kept grading by letter.

My fiancé, Jonathan Knight, was the first and only one in Cassie's system to receive an A. And he got it before the second date. Needless to say, no one ranked an A+. The chance of any guy rating that high was not likely. To deserve an A+, Jonathan needed to score A's in all categories *and* have the ability to pick all five correct lotto numbers plus the Powerball.

At the outset, Cassie had comprised a checklist to assist her in rating my dates, and Jonathan was the first to have all the boxes checked. And a double check was worth four checks.

Intelligent—check.
Grounded—check.
Commonsensical—check.
Loving—check.
Spiritual—check.
Funny—check.
Hot looking—check.

Didn't get handsy—check.

While on a date, didn't sneak a peek at the playoff game on his phone—check.

Didn't eat with his mouth open—check.

Paid for the meal—check.

Left a tip—check.

Didn't insist on coming up for "coffee"—check.

Didn't wait two weeks to call again—check.

Mentioned that best friend Cassie was smart and beautiful too—check check.

I stood in front of the mirror and turned from side to side, examining my dress—a straightforward, chiffon, A-line style. "The decision to go ankle-length was smart—it'll work perfectly in the sand. The only thing my mother will be happy about is I'll be barefoot during the ceremony. She'll think that's cool. Jonathan and I will both be barefoot."

Cassie raised one brow. "Does Jonathan know about this?"

In the few months since we met, I've learned to feed him information a little at a time. "Not yet. He's probably having his wingtip dress shoes shined at this very moment."

Cassie flashed a wry smile. "Yeah, he'll loosen up. Sure."

The thought of Jonathan loosening up made me grin. "You're being sarcastic. So you don't think I can change him? You don't think I can get him to loosen up?"

"Uh, no."

I lowered my voice. "My goal is to get him to agree to something really romantic. Like tattooing each other's initials in a discreet location, like on our butt cheeks—a place that only he and I will know."

"Right, only the two of you—and now *me*," Cassie said, looking repulsed. "That's a bit of TMI that I could've done without."

CHAPTER 2

Jonathan told me he would be a few blocks away in a men's clothing store to have a tailor pin the hemline of his pants. Jonathan was meticulous about his suit and dragged his best man, Howie, with him to make sure Howie's suit looked impeccable too.

I closed my eyes for a moment and envisioned how that scene might be unfolding. Jonathan was most likely informing the tailor that the pant leg should fall onto the top of his polished dress shoes—but not too much. Or complaining that when he lifts his arms to chest-level, there's an unacceptable gap between the suit jacket's back collar and the shirt's collar. I shook my head and giggled a bit at that scene in my head. Without a doubt, Howie is surely seated a few feet away in a chair, throwing his head back, and laughing at Jonathan's instructions to the tailor. I can see it all.

Cassie's voice brought me back to the moment. "I'm so happy for you," she said. "This was all meant to be. This truly is a love-at-first-sight story."

I tried not to smile too much, but I couldn't help it. "I knew he was *the one* the first minute I laid eyes on him. And he says the same about me. Funny thing, when you instantly fall head over heels, it seems like nothing else matters. In the few short months we've known each other, I know there's still so much to learn about him. And I'm fine with letting those puzzle pieces fall into place as time goes on."

"That is totally unlike you, girl."

My grin grew broader. "I know."

The bridal stylist entered with Cassie's bridesmaid's dress.

Cassie said to me, "You haven't been yourself since you met him. Everything you've done is out of character."

"Maybe. But maybe he brings out the real me."

"No. The things you've been doing lately are not the real you."

If Cassie were on the witness stand, I'd object. "Cass, I'm afraid your argument lacks foundation and assumes facts not in evidence."

"Please don't talk like I'm an opposing attorney. You know I hate that."

"Sorry. I'm trying to break that habit."

Cassie smirked. "You want evidence that you're not yourself these days? How about the way you proposed to Jonathan?"

I chuckled. "You mean flying the banner?"

The stylist asked, "*You* proposed?"

Shrugging my shoulders, I answered, "Somebody had to. Jonathan's way too cautious to pop the question after only a couple of months."

Cassie put her hand over her mouth to hide her laugh. "Tell her how you proposed."

The stylist sat next to Cassie on the loveseat, folded her arms, and stared intently at me.

Heat suddenly radiated from what must have been my flushed face. What I was about to reveal was an idea that, at the time, seemed exciting. But hearing myself retell it to a stranger who wasn't part of that magic moment somehow turns my supposed romantic idea into a cringe-worthy and cheesy stunt. I swallowed hard and said, "I hired an airplane to fly a banner that read: Will you marry me, J?"

The stylist peered over the top of her glasses. "J?"

"I used only his first name initial because Jonathan is a very discreet person. He wouldn't want his name to be flaunted publicly like that."

Cassie turned to the stylist and said, "Actually, spelling out Jonathan was another four hundred bucks."

"Don't listen to her. Cost was not a factor."

"I remember Howie called your fiancé *J* for a week," Cassie said.

"Howie?" asked the stylist.

"The best man." I said.

Cassie clarified. "Well, not the best man, but the only one Jonathan could find."

Waving off Cassie's remark, I said to the stylist, "Don't believe her. Howie's a good man."

"Piper, tell her the real reason you proposed using *J* instead of Jonathan."

Before explaining, I shook my head, uttered a slight laugh, and lowered my voice. "Well, jokingly I told Cassie that if Jonathan said no, I was going to fly the banner over my ex-boyfriend's house—Jeremiah."

Cassie and the stylist chuckled.

"A girl always needs a back-up plan," I added.

They laughed again.

The stylist's brows raised. "You weren't really going to do that, were you?"

I shook my head while still giggling.

The stylist said, "I bet he responded in an equally unique and romantic way."

I paused and turned to Cassie. I didn't have to answer because Cassie was all too willing to answer that one.

Cassie turned to the stylist. "Yeah. He responded. By fax."

In a defensive tone, I added, "He was at work."

"Fax? Who has a fax machine these days?" the stylist asked.

"Not me," I said. "So, the fax that never reached me apparently said *yes*. And that's my fiancé for ya. He's a little bit old school. There's nothing like sweeping a girl off her feet with obsolete, outdated technology."

Cassie laughed. "The telegraph lines must have been down that day."

The stylist and Cassie both laughed.

"Okay. Okay. He's not perfect," I said. "But the tiny flaws I'm discovering are easily fixable."

Cassie shook her head. "And there you go. The future Mrs. Knight's famous last words."

"Knight?" the stylist asked. "Is your fiancé Jonathan Knight? The Jonathan Knight running for Congress?"

As Cassie grabbed her bridesmaid's dress and headed to the dressing room, I answered the stylist. "Yes. That's my guy." I was ecstatic when she recognized his name. Jonathan wasn't doing too well in the polls, but if this stylist knew his name, things had to be looking up.

Jonathan was running against the unethical incumbent, Malcom Hyde, for the Congressional seat in the 24th district. Hyde had been a fixture in that seat for decades and had everyone in his back pocket. Most experts gave Jonathan no chance of winning. Unseating Malcom Hyde was a task Jonathan was not eager to undertake, but the sleazy congressman's corrupt ways were despicable enough that someone had to take a stand. Jonathan eventually became determined to give the citizens a representative they could be proud of. Someone that would lend stability back to the district.

Jonathan's first decision was to choose his best friend, Howie, as his campaign manager. So, Howie must've been doing something right if Jonathan's name was getting out there.

Cassie shuffled out of a changing room wearing her new mermaid-style bridesmaid dress. In a tone that showed she was not amused, Cassie pointed to the wide-brimmed denim fedora on her head and asked, "Uh, what's with the hat?"

Clearing my throat, I said, "It's a small tribute to my mother."

Dead silence from Cassie.

"No?"

Cassie put her hands on her hips. "No."

I needed to distract Cassie from the hat and the mermaid-style dress and get her out of the bridal shop. "We're meeting Jonathan for lunch."

"I'm skipping lunch today."

"Why?"

"That mermaid dress. I can't afford to gain another pound. Eating is not a priority for me right now."

"That's too bad. Lunch is on Jonathan."

"Free food is still fattening. Dating taught me that."

"Suit yourself." I stood up. "But we're supposed to meet him at the Dock House."

"The Dock House? I love that place! But no. No way. I can't eat a thing today."

"I'll tell Jonathan and Howie you said hello."

Cassie grabbed my arm. "Howie will be there?"

"Yep."

Her left eyebrow raised, and her lips lifted upward at the corners. "You didn't tell me Howie would join us."

"I didn't think it mattered."

"No, it matters. Howie's hot."

I froze while my brain tried to make sense of her words. The phrase *Howie's hot* was not something I ever expected to hear—at least not from a sober woman. I turned to Cassie. "Hot? I'm talking about Jonathan's friend, Howie. *That* Howie."

"I know," she said, her eyes twinkling. "There's only one Howie."

I shook my head. "You can say that again."

We parked and approached the restaurant named The Dock House. It was built at the edge of the beach between two bluffs. Palm fronds waved in the afternoon breeze, and nearby crashing waves filled the air. The late morning sun was mild and provided the perfect temperature for lunching outdoors. A hostess escorted us to a patio filled with blue umbrella-covered tables at the edge of the sand. The sparkling Pacific Ocean was our backdrop.

Jonathan and Howie sat at the far edge of the patio. As we approached, Jonathan stood up to greet us. He was as handsome as ever. The breeze playfully ruffled his brown hair with natural highlights from the sun. The color of his stubble beard was brown but darker, accentuating his strong jawline. He had rolled the sleeves of his white shirt half-way up his arms and, as we kissed hello, my hands touched his toned forearms. He gently pressed his lips against mine, sending electric tingles throughout my body.

Howie, wearing his ball cap to hide his thinning hair, stood to say hello to Cassie and me. As he rose, he bumped into the table and tipped his glass of iced tea on its side. Half of the freezing tea splashed across the front of my jeans while a much lesser amount dripped down Cassie's bare arm.

"I'm so sorry!" Howie said to Cassie as he grabbed a cloth napkin from the table. "I'll wipe it off."

Cassie smiled. "No biggie. A few drops of tea on my arm won't kill me."

"I insist," he said. Howie quickly wiped her arm with the napkin.

I stood there, shocked, looking down at the front of my soaked jeans with my arms held out and away from my sides.

Howie and Cassie sat down in their seats and locked eyes.

"I'm very sorry," he said to her.

She dismissed his concern with a wave of her hand. "It's nothing. No worries."

I cleared my throat, but they paid no attention.

Jonathan picked up another napkin, but before he wiped the front of my jeans, he froze. "Piper, I can't dry you off there."

"People will talk," I said.

I grabbed the napkin and dabbed my jeans the best I could.

"I'm sorry that happened," Jonathan said, glancing toward Howie. But Howie was engrossed in his conversation with Cassie and paid no attention to my drenched jeans.

"Maybe the weather will dry me off."

A waitress approached and picked up the empty glass from the table. "Is everything alright?"

Jonathan glanced up at her. "We had a little spill."

Howie, oblivious to the spill he caused, turned to grab his glass of tea. When he noticed it was gone, he said, "Oh, I guess I'll need another iced tea."

I turned on my most sarcastic tone and said, "It's on me, Howie."

Howie shook his head. "Not necessary. Jonathan's buying today."

"That's not what I meant."

His perplexed facial expression convinced me to drop it and move on.

"I'll have a glass of water, please," I told the waitress.

"I'll be right back with that water," she said.

"Jonathan, I think I have an extra pair of shorts in my trunk. I'll be right back."

Howie turned toward me as I walked away. "Piper, where ya going?"

"To change."

Howie shook his head. "Women. I'll never understand 'em."

As luck would have it, I had a shopping bag of honeymoon clothes still in my car's trunk. I rifled through them and found a pair of white Capri pants.

I changed in the restaurant's restroom and rejoined the others at our table.

Cassie turned to me with an eager tone in her voice. "Piper. Good. You're back! Howie was just telling us about the fitting session they had at the men's store. Tell her, Howie!"

Howie took a deep breath. "Okay. Okay—"

Cassie held up her hand to stop Howie. "Hey, wait a minute. Piper, those weren't the pants you had on earlier."

I turned and stared at Jonathan without saying a word. He leaned closer to me and whispered, "If these two ever hook up, they could be perfect for each other."

Faster than Howie will spill a drink, I replied, "Ya think?"

"Today's trip to the clothing store was so Jonathan," Howie said. "Get this. He tries on a coat, raises his elbows out like this, and says, 'When I do this, there's an unacceptable gap between the coat collar and shirt collar.' Who does that?"

I knew it! That's exactly what Jonathan would say, because he said it to me when trying on suit coats at his house.

With a tiny smirk, I turned to Jonathan and asked, "What? No instructions on where the pant leg should fall on the shoe?"

Howie just about came out of his chair. "Yes! He said that too! I couldn't believe how finicky he was. I asked him, 'How did you get like this?' But that was a rhetorical question. I know *exactly* how he got like this."

Jonathan responded, "Leave my dad out of this."

Howie laughed. "Well, I'm glad you at least know what's behind your anal personality."

Jonathan frowned. "I hate that word."

Howie chuckled again. "And that's because you're anal."

Jonathan lowered his voice to ensure no one heard their conversation's crude direction. "I prefer the word *persnickety*."

Howie leaned toward me. "Piper, do you realize you're marrying a dude who uses the word *persnickety*?"

I put my head on Jonathan's shoulder. "Yes, and I like that word too."

Jonathan shook his head. "Alright. Real funny. Look, just because I have good taste in clothing—"

Howie cut in. "You should've said, 'Good taste in *women*,'" He nodded toward me.

And that comment almost made up for spilling his iced tea on me. Almost.

Leaning closer to Jonathan, I said, "I think I'm getting to know all your cute little quirks and habits."

On her way past our table, the waitress set a glass of water in front of me.

Jonathan picked up my hand. "At first I thought we should take more time to get to know each other before getting married, but I'm thinking that whole thing might be over-rated."

I agreed. "Nothing wrong with a little mystery."

"Jonathan," Howie started, "should I bring up the other subject we talked about at the men's store? This might be a good time to find out."

"Howie, what is wrong with you?" Jonathan asked.

Though Jonathan and Howie had been best friends since the fourth grade, Jonathan has commented several times that he couldn't remember exactly why they became close friends in the first place. Temperamentally, they were as different as night and day. As loyal a friend as Howie was, Jonathan said he sometimes was more of an irritant that never quite goes away—much like jock itch.

Cassie asked, "What subject did you two talk about today?"

Jonathan glanced at Howie and made a slashing motion across his neck as a sign to cut the conversation.

Howie ignored him. "Hey, Piper. We were trying to remember that ex-boyfriend's name you mentioned the last time we all got together. What was that name again?"

"Why do you want to know that?" I asked.

"No reason, really," Howie answered. "We were just talking about old flames. So, what was his name?"

"Andrew. Why?"

"No, that wasn't it. It was a longer name. The last guy you were kinda serious about."

Jonathan interrupted. "Howie, just drop it."

"Jeremiah," Cassie said. "Her last boyfriend was Jeremiah."

Howie's lips tightened as if he was suppressing a laugh. "You were right, Jonathan."

"Right about what?" I asked.

"I told him he was crazy," Howie said. "He thought you used only a *J* on that plane's banner in case you need a Plan B. Jonathan thought that if he turned you down, the plane would continue on to your last boyfriend's house."

I turned to Jonathan, who was in the process of slouching in his chair in an effort to disappear.

"We were joking, that's all," Jonathan said. "Tell her, Howie. We were just joking."

I crossed my arms. "Well, I don't think that's something to joke around about."

Upon hearing those words, Cassie's head jerked in my direction.

I needed to change the subject. I reached for my water and somehow knocked the entire contents into Howie's lap while I said, "Don't forget, Jonathan. My free-spirited Mother is flying in for the wedding today."

I'm not certain if it was the cold water I knocked onto Howie's lap or me mentioning the impending arrival of my wack-a-doodle Mother, but no one brought up my ex-boyfriend again that day.

CHAPTER 3

I stood in my Santa Barbara condo's kitchen, deciding what to drink. Iced tea had lost its appeal at the moment, so I grabbed a glass of wine and headed to the den where Jonathan sat. His eyes were glued to the TV and pointing the remote control at the screen.

I offered a friendly tip. "You know, once you decide on the channel, you don't have to point the remote anymore."

He didn't respond.

As he fixated on the news, I studied him. What a sweetie he was to not criticize the interior decorating. One look around provided plenty of opportunities for mockery, yet he barely uttered a word. Granted, my condo looked traditional on the outside—Spanish architecture, a red tile roof, dark wood trim, white stucco. But the décor my fiancé was sitting in the middle of was anything but traditional, to put it mildly.

My mother, Harmony, as a gift, had just transformed the condo's interior from soothing earth tones to a bold bohemian décor. She used a broad palette of colors, including turquoise, deep reds, greens, blues, purples, yellows, and a few hues even Sherwin Williams couldn't name. She replaced my sleek, minimalist furniture with an eclectic mix of styles best described as either vintage, gaudy, thrift shop, or yard sale. Large throw pillows of various colors, daybeds, and lounges filled every room. The wallpaper throughout the home had a theme: clutter. The living room walls were deep green and peppered with bright red roses. Tapestry rugs hung on most walls, and Turkish lamps, lamps with macrame shades, and a slew of candles provided the lighting. I tried my best to be positive and hoped it would grow on me—in a non-fungal way, of course.

Jonathan most likely ignored the over-the-top decorating, knowing he only had to endure it for a few more days. We both agreed that after the wedding, I would move to his nearby home in Montecito—a home where dinner guests could visit without the feeling of being trapped inside a broken kaleidoscope.

I sat next to Jonathan and rubbed his back. "Two more days until the wedding! Can you believe it?"

Jonathan remained silent, concentrating on the local TV news channel.

I tried again. "I spent my whole life dreaming about my wedding day. I feel like a real-life Cinderella."

Still no response.

Using my biggest smile, I said, "My prince has arrived."

Jonathan turned up the volume on the remote.

My smile disappeared. With no emotion except for a slight hint of sarcasm, I said, "I must be dreaming. Pinch me."

Still, nothing I said broke Jonathan's concentration.

"Jonathan!"

He re-pointed the remote at the TV. "Shhhh. They're about to do a story on my campaign."

"Did you just shush me? You did. This is not happening. Oh hell no."

I grabbed the remote from his hand and muted the sound.

"Piper, what are you doing?"

He took back the remote and unmuted the sound.

"Jonathan, is this how it will be when we're old? Fighting over the remote?"

"Don't be silly," he said. "When we're old, we won't know how to work a remote."

"Oh, real funny. Just listen to me. You won't miss a thing. I'm recording that news show. But for now, I'm trying to talk to you." I wrestled the remote from him and pointed it at the TV. "I'm switching to The Wedding Channel."

Jonathan leaned back. "Okay. Okay. I'll listen. But don't change the channel. I still want to see this news story about me and my campaign as it's being aired. I'm a little stressed. Running for congress and getting married at the same time is making me a little crazy. So, I'm sorry. I'm all ears. What is it you need to talk about?"

"Thank you. I want to talk about our wedding. Half the fun is the anticipation. And it's almost here." Holding my hand in the air, I stared at the back of my fingers. "I'll be wearing a wedding ring in two days." I leaned against him. "And you'll have a wedding ring, too." His left hand was on his knee, so I placed my hand next to his. "That's weird. Look at that."

"Look at what?"

"Our middle fingers. They're both longer than the others."

"All middle fingers are longer than the others."

I tilted my head to study our hands. "Oh, so now you're an expert in middle fingers?"

"I used to commute to L.A. I've seen plenty of them."

I tried not to laugh but did anyway.

He turned toward me. "That can't be what you wanted to talk about."

"Right. It's not. What I wanted to tell you is—"

Jonathan interrupted her and pointed to the TV. "That's just great. Fantastic," he said sarcastically. "They bumped my story with an update on the naked strangler story. Can you believe that? A naked guy sneaking around, trying to strangle people. That's your top story these days."

"*Alleged* naked strangler," I said.

Jonathan shook his head at the TV. "And that's why I'm running for office. We've got to protect the public from guys like that."

While changing the channel, I said, "He's still presumed innocent until proven guilty, you know."

"What are you? His lawyer?" he scoffed.

Except for feigning a laugh, I didn't respond.

He said, "So, tell me what's on your mind."

"Okay. Promise me you won't get mad."

He kissed my cheek. "You could never make me mad. You know that."

I had one eye on the Wedding Channel. "Okay. Well…" I turned up the TV volume. "Look at that wedding cake!"

He took the remote and lowered the volume. "Don't change the subject. Now, what is it you need to tell me?"

I was the one who wanted to engage in a conversation. Now, I'm not so sure the timing was right. I turned toward him but avoided eye contact. "You know I'm under a lot of pressure at work. And because I'm new in the Public Defender's office, I'm not in a position to turn down any case they might give me."

"Go on."

"Well, with our wedding coming up, they had the nerve to assign a new case to me. Can you believe that?"

Jonathan smiled. "No biggie. Work on it when we get back from our honeymoon. We'll only be gone a few days."

I wrapped my arms around him and kissed him all over his face. "Thank you, sweetie. I knew you'd understand."

"That was it? That's what was so important?"

"Pretty much."

He leaned back and studied my face. "What do you mean by *pretty much*?"

My interest in The Wedding Channel intensified. I turned up the volume again. "Wow! Look at all those grooms wearing tuxedos!"

Jonathan grabbed the remote and turned the volume down. "Piper?"

My eyes were now riveted to the screen. "Look at those guys. Nice cummerbunds."

"Stop checking out their cummerbunds—whatever that is—and be straight with me. I'm guessing there's more to your story."

I rested my chin in my hand and pointed my eyes at the ceiling to make it look like I was trying to remember something. "Okay.

Let me think. What in the heck was it I wanted to tell you? Hmmm. I guess I forgot. No, wait. Yes, I remember now."

"Just say it."

I grimaced, closed my eyes, and blurted, "I'm defending the Naked Strangler."

Jonathan jumped up from the sofa. "No no no no no no no no no no no no!"

When I opened my eyes, he was stomping around the room. "I'm getting the feeling you're against it."

He paced the floor. "Piper, you can't do this to me!"

"This is not about you. It's about me and my job. I happen to work in the Public Defender's office, and sometimes we don't defend perfect people."

"I know that. But the Naked Strangler? Why can't you defend somebody else? Like someone who crossed the street where there's no crosswalk."

"I am. They nabbed him while he was jaywalking."

Jonathan plopped down on the sofa and rubbed his head as if he had a headache. "When I first met you, I knew you were an attorney, but I had no idea you were *this* kind of attorney."

"The kind that defends the innocent?"

"Then defend the innocent! Not a naked guy walking around with a long…"

I folded my arms. "A long what?"

"A long… rap sheet."

"News flash! He's innocent until proven guilty."

Jonathan tried to lower his voice and calm down. "Do I need to remind you I'm running on a platform of law and order, making the streets safe, bringing back decency?"

"I'm not stopping you."

"How's this going to look? I'm trying to project a certain image, and my new wife is—"

"Tread lightly. I'm not your wife yet."

"Are you saying you might back out of this wedding?"

"Depends on how this goes." I put on a tough front, but there was no way I'd back out of the wedding.

"Well, I just don't want my wife defending the Naked Strangler."

"*Alleged* Naked Strangler," I said. "Wait. Correction. Naked for sure; alleged strangler."

Jonathan frowned. "Please rethink this, Piper. Defending this nude nutcase is a mistake. Law-abiding citizens have the right to walk down the street without a gun pointed at them."

"That was no gun."

"All I know is Congressman Hyde is going to have a field day with this."

An alarm on my phone beeped, and I stood. "We'll finish this later. We have to pick up my mother at the airport."

Jonathan and I were driving toward the arrival area of LAX.

I sneaked a glance at Jonathan out of the corner of my eye. I had that weird urge to swallow before I spoke. I have no idea why, but every time I dread having to say something or talk about an uncomfortable subject, I have this big swallow to get out of the way. It's weird because I must swallow all day long and never notice any of them. But this is one of those moments, so I swallowed. "You finally get to meet my mother. She's a little different—kind of a free spirit. But you two should get along fine. Remember, she's from a long line of hippies, so if you keep that in mind, everything she does will make more sense."

"Then, technically, *you're* from a long line of hippies."

I thought about that, and my shoulders slumped. "Guilty as charged."

Jonathan had that look like he was trying to interpret my facial expression. "You don't look excited to see your mother."

"Look, I love my mother, I really do. But she's anti-wedding and anti-marriage. I'd rather she visit another time. This will not be easy."

"I get it," Jonathan said. "She's the type that hates men."

"You're wrong there. She loves men and has always had a man in her life. She just never married, and I think she's bitter about that."

"What was the problem?"

"Too much time elapsed between the first date and the wedding. The men got to know her and every one of them backed out." My mouth formed a sly grin. "She should've scheduled a quick wedd—" I stopped talking.

His eyes widened. "That's why our quick engagement? So we'll be married before I really get to know you?"

"Hey, I'm still getting to know you too. Don't be silly. Anyway, we're talking about my mother. In her life, Mr. Right always turned into Mr. Wrong. And it wasn't all her fault. She backed out plenty of times. In fact, most of the times it was my mother who called off the wedding."

Sugar-coating this information served no purpose. I owed it to Jonathan to tell him the truth about her. My mother would always find something in every man that irked her. Sometimes, she'd discover a minor detail at the last minute—like her fiance's recent completion of a twenty-year prison sentence for attempting to bomb the state capital. Other times, she would discover a serious flaw—like his longing for a house in the suburbs with a white picket fence.

Jonathan glanced at me with a wrinkled brow. "So, Harmony thinks you're walking right into a suffocating, evil institution called marriage?"

"Probably."

Jonathan reached over and touched my hand. "I'm so sorry. Marriage is the foundation of our society. It's a good thing. My parents loved being married and celebrated every anniversary like it was the most important thing in the world."

I became lost in my thoughts and stared out the window. I truly did want to be honest with him, but too much Harmony-related information might scare him off. He said his parents celebrated plenty of anniversaries, but I dare not mention that my mother had plenty of anniversaries too. Anniversaries of break-ups and wedding cancelations. Several times a year, she would bake a wedding cake topped with a plastic bride—minus the groom. I remember it all like it was yesterday. My mother would cut the cake and shout, "Dodged that one!" Then she'd shout a particular date and year. Depending on which canceled wedding she celebrated, a plastic groom might appear on the cake but never next to the bride. Sometimes the groom would be inserted headfirst into the bottom layer with only his legs protruding, and other times the groom would lie twisted at the base of the cake with his legs broken. The plastic groom's unfortunate position on the cake matched the intensity of the breakup. And sometimes, the groom was missing altogether.

I placed my hand on Jonathan's upper arm. "I just need to keep her involvement to a minimum. This wedding is the most important thing in my life, and I will not let her ruin it."

"I'm sure she'll be fine," Jonathan said.

"She did promise me she'll try to have a good attitude about it all."

As we approached the curbside pickup area, a woman who—I'll be diplomatic here—wore interesting clothing, waved at us.

"Oh, my God. Let me guess. That's her," Jonathan said.

CHAPTER 4

Jonathan's car veered across two lanes and pulled to the airport's curb.

"That's the one and only Harmony," I said, glancing at Jonathan to see his reaction. "By the way, don't mention the Naked Strangler case to my mother."

Jonathan nodded. "Fine. Will it frighten her?"

"No, it'll excite her."

My mother, around fifty years old, was grinning from ear to ear. She was wearing a broad-brimmed hat, harem pants, a shawl with long fringe, over-sized round purple sunglasses, an off-the-shoulder renaissance-style top, bejeweled sandals, a long leather necklace from which hung a hubcap-sized eyesore posing as crocheted artwork, an over-sized orange scarf wrapped around her neck, and a half-dozen bracelets on each wrist. She had auburn hair in the front, but it transitioned to a blueish tint near the back of her head. On the ground next to her were two large carpet bags.

Jonathan and I exited the car. He popped open the trunk while I reached out with both arms to hug my mother.

My mother excitedly ran in-place and screamed, "You got the Naked Strangler case!"

We embraced while I asked, "How did you—forget it. Let's talk about that later."

She winked. "Just call me when they do the police line-up."

"Too late, Mother. It already took place."

My mother put her hands on her hips. "Piper, we've been through this too many times. Please call me Harmony. You know I never liked *Mother*." Her body shivered at the thought. "It's way too domesticated."

Ever since I became an adult, she says she feels old when I call her mother. She wants people to think we're sisters. I'll keep using *Mother*.

She tilted her head at Jonathan before turning to me. "So, this is him. This is your Johnny."

"Glad to meet you," he said. "I've heard a lot about you."

"Don't believe half of what you've heard," she said, while slapping him on his ass. "Believe *all* of it."

Jonathan tried to shake her hand, but she pushed his hand to the side and wrapped her arms around him.

"He goes by Jonathan, not Johnny," I said.

My mother glanced back at me and crinkled her nose. "The name *Jonathan* sounds snooty." She bent her neck back to gaze up at his face and asked, "Can I call you *Johnny*?"

"I'd rather you didn't," he said. "Jonathan is what everyone calls me."

"And don't call him J, either," I said. "He has a problem with that, too."

My mother took a step back. "Let me take a look at what swept Piper off her feet." Her top lip on one side of her mouth raised ever so slightly as she examined him from head to toe. "Interesting threads. Let me guess," she said, "you sell vacation timeshares."

"Mother, Jonathan's an attorney. That's how we met."

My mother's brows pointed down. "Oh, that's right. Lawyers in love." In a flat tone, she added, "How romantic."

Jonathan placed her two carpet bags into the trunk. My mother sat in the back seat, and Jonathan and I climbed back into the front seats.

As Jonathan drove, I asked, "How was your trip, Mother?"

"It seems like I just left San Francisco a few minutes ago. Air travel is such a miracle."

Given her excessively accessorized outfit, Jonathan thought the real miracle was that she got through the airport metal detector.

I twisted my body enough to make eye contact with her when we spoke. "I couldn't wait for you to meet the love of my life. Isn't he perfect?"

"Well, they say there's someone for everyone," she answered. "He just needs a wardrobe tweak, that's all—sandals, beads—you know." She leaned forward, closer to him. "I have one word for you, Jonathan."

"I want to know," he said in a disingenuous tone.

"Turquoise."

"What?"

"Turquoise. It'll open up a whole new world for you."

Jonathan half-smiled. "Piper, help me remember that tip. I don't want to forget it."

"You won't," I said with a smirk. "She'll remind you." I bit one side of my lower lip in preparation for my next bit of news. "By the way, Mother, you're going to meet Jonathan's dad tomorrow at a luncheon. We'll all be there."

"Is he anything like Jonathan?"

"Exactly like him."

In a monotone voice, she said, "I'm not sure I can stand the excitement."

I explained. "Walter isn't exactly the fun type. He's a serious, no-nonsense type of guy. Don't get me wrong, he's a nice man, just not the life of the party—if you know what I mean."

"Sounds like he's coming off a bad divorce."

Jonathan glanced at me and remained silent.

"Mother, Jonathan's mom passed away several years ago."

She reached forward and placed her hand on Jonathan's shoulder. "I'm so sorry, J. That's a bummer."

"Thank you; I appreciate that."

"So, Piper, what does Jonathan's father think of how I decorated your condo?"

"He hasn't seen it yet. In the few months Jonathan and I have been seeing each other, I've only met him twice, and he's never been to my home. Anyway, he's gone through a lot. I don't blame him for not being the life of the party."

She faced the window and mumbled, "Tomorrow ought to be a real hoot."

We finally arrived at my condo. While I was unlocking the front door, my mother grabbed Jonathan's hand and examined his palm.

Jonathan didn't know how to react due to a lifetime of experiencing very few spontaneous palm readings. "Can I ask what you're doing?"

She ignored his question and continued looking at the lines of his palm. "Okay… Huh… That's odd." Then, a troubled look appeared on her face. "Hmmm."

"Is there a problem?"

"Well, honestly. Kind of a drag, really. But we'll get back to this later."

I pushed open the door, and we stepped inside. Jonathan followed, still looking at his palm.

The condo's interior made my mother's eyes light up, and she put her hand on her heart. "It's just as lovely as the day I decorated it! Then she stopped and scratched her head. "Where's the huge Lady Godiva painting I gave you?"

My heart pounded upon hearing her question. I forgot I gave it to Cassie a few months earlier—about the time I met Jonathan. I didn't want to scare him off with such a vivid painting. Lady Godiva being nude wasn't the issue—Jonathan could've handled that—but the portrait lacked historic accuracy. The unknown artist of this painting augmented Godiva's breasts as if she rode the horse straight from Beverly Hills, gave her full lips enhanced by Botox, and tattooed her in places that would cause a jaded tattoo artist to blush. Cassie took the portrait home, marked it as free, and put it by the curb. However, a homeless person returned it the next day.

Still, my mother's question needed answering. And there's that urge to swallow hard again. I didn't want to lie, but her feelings needed to be protected, so I had to say something. "Mother, Cassie would comment on that painting every time she came over. She said it made her jaw drop. So, it was around her birthday when I gave it to her because she mentioned once that she had the perfect spot for it. I told Cassie it's from you and she couldn't give that away even if she wanted to. And so far, she still has it. She still can't believe she's its owner. She stares at it and shakes her head every time she leaves her house."

My mother turned to Jonathan and said, "You would've loved it—her long hair flowing, riding through town bareback. It was striking."

"When you say *bareback*, you mean no saddle?" Jonathan asked.

She shook her head at Jonathan. "No. *Lady Godiva* was bare. Who cares what the horse was wearing?" She turned back toward me. "Speaking of Cassie, how's she doing?"

"She's good," I answered. "You'll see her at the rehearsal."

Jonathan had a worried expression. "Cassie's not a re-gifter, is she?"

I ignored Jonathan's acerbic question. "Anyway, Mother, that's what happened. Not a day goes by that I don't look at that wall and notice it's gone." I nodded unconvincingly at Jonathan. "You would've really thought that painting was something, honey."

"I'll get you another one right away," she said.

I relaxed. The chances of her acquiring another painting at that moment was an impossibility—it was after 5 p.m., and the swap meet was closed.

My mother studied the room. "It's a large painting. Where would I put it?"

It would have been easy for Jonathan to suggest where to put it, but kept his mouth shut.

"Mother, it's too nice of a gift to buy twice. Don't worry about it."

"Don't be silly. I'll throw it in with the deal when I do

Jonathan's place."

Jonathan shot me a look of deadly seriousness. "What's she talking about?"

I faced Jonathan and cocked my head to one side. "Did I forget to mention this to you? My mother wants to decorate your home in Montecito—I mean, our home—as a wedding gift. Can I get you a drink? How 'bout whiskey?"

Jonathan glared at me.

"I know," my mother said to Jonathan, "you're speechless. But don't you worry. I can do the same thing to your place. It comes naturally to me. No formal training—all instinct."

Jonathan looked around the room. "You can't teach this look," he said.

"Jonathan…" I cautioned.

As my mother headed to the restroom, she said, "I guess I got my decorating skills from my own mother. Excuse me; I gotta pee."

As soon as she was out of earshot, Jonathan asked, "Her mother? Piper, your grandmother was like Harmony?"

"Exactly like her."

"Wow." Jonathan stood there, thinking. "If we ever do one of those ancestry DNA tests, we'll trace my roots back centuries to some faraway country and *yours* no further than Woodstock."

My shoulders slumped. "I know."

Jonathan walked to where I was standing and hugged me. "I'm sorry. It's this political campaign I'm going through. It's making me crazy."

My stomach churned. "You want to call off the wedding, don't you?"

He kissed me on the forehead. "Of course not. I love you."

What a sweetie. No wonder I love him so much. "Let's just try to get through this. I know my mother is unique. She is. She's different. I've always known it."

Jonathan nodded. "She's probably normal in ways I haven't seen yet, I'm sure."

"Uh, the date printed on her bank checks is *The Age of*

Aquarius."

"You're right. She *is* different." Jonathan embraced me tightly. "How you turned out halfway sane, I'll never know."

"Halfway? Is that a compliment?" I closed my eyes and rested my head on his shoulder. "Try to go easy on her. Her childhood was unconventional, to say the least. She was raised in a Volkswagen bus and was eighteen before she learned that not every vehicle comes with shag carpeting and a guitar. And that's part of who I am. I was raised by a single mother who was raised by a single mother. I come from a long line of women who never quite got that wedding ring. But that won't be *my* story. Our marriage will end that unfortunate trend once and for all."

CHAPTER 5

My mother came out of the bathroom and headed to the kitchen.

Jonathan stood at the window and scrutinized the street below.

"Do you see something down there?" I asked.

"I'm looking for reporters. I'm sure Hyde is trying to find some dirt on me." He continued to scan the street. "We can never be too careful, you know."

I walked to the window and stood next to him. "People think you're grounded and full of common sense, but I know the real truth. You're a little paranoid. Still, I love you to death." I wrapped my arms around him and kissed his lips.

He pulled back. "Piper! What are you doing?"

"If I have to explain a kiss to you, you're going to need an instruction booklet on our wedding night."

"You don't understand. It's not so much the kiss; it's kissing in front of the window."

I nodded, as if he was making perfect sense. "I can see the headline now. Man Kisses Fiancé in Window. Political Career Destroyed." I turned and walked away, shaking my head.

He blurted, "It could happen."

"Come away from the window, Jonathan, and help me light some candles. You're acting paranoid."

"Hey, when a reliable source tells you my opponent is having us surveilled, I take it seriously."

"Jonathan, I need a hand lighting candles."

"*You* light them. I'm searching the street below for paparazzi or anyone gathering intelligence."

"If they're gathering actual intelligence around here, they'll be disappointed."

"Right there!" he said. "Look by the dumpster."

I peered at the street below. "That's the trash man."

"So we think."

I squinted through the window. "Oh, no. What if he discovers we put pineapple on our pizza?"

"Stop joking, Piper. We don't know if he's a real trash man or not."

"I'm guessing he is. The thirty-foot trash truck looks legit."

Something made him close the drapes. He took a breath, parted the curtains a few inches with his hands, and peeked out. "Who is that? I've never seen her before."

I opened the drapes enough to peek out.

He snapped the drapes shut. "Piper, they'll see you."

I raised one eyebrow and opened the drapes again. "The girl on the bicycle? That's Chrissy. She sold us Girl Scout cookies a month ago."

"She did? Where's that cookie box? It might be bugged."

I calmly turned and walked away. "Too late. I ate them. I guess Chrissy never guessed you'd catch on to her career in political espionage. She'll have to take things up a notch. Now, will you help me light these candles?"

Jonathan ignored me and kept an eye on the street.

"Never mind. I'll do it myself."

I headed to the kitchen, where I retrieved a candle-lighting tool from the drawer. I moved through the apartment and lit as many as I could.

Jonathan took a break from surveilling the street for cookie-peddling spies and turned his attention to watching the candle-lighting frenzy. "What are you doing?" he asked.

"Lighting candles."

"Why?"

"So, they'll be lit."

"My dad's going to see your condo, eventually. Maybe any day now. He'll think a home with this many lighted candles is weird."

My mother walked into the living room. "Everyone digs candles."

"Not him," Jonathan said. "Especially this many. He'll think we're going to sacrifice something."

I continued to move from one candle to another, lighting them. I didn't know it at the time, but Jonathan was right behind me, blowing them out.

"Your dad will like it," I said, without looking back at Jonathan.

"He won't. Trust me."

"He'll think it's cozy."

Jonathan shook his head. "He'll think it's cultish."

"Don't they smell good, Mother?"

My mother smiled. "Lavender! I love lavender."

"I chose this aroma for its calming properties."

Jonathan put his hand to his forehead. "Is it for my dad if he shows up? You think he'll need a calming aroma?"

"Not for your dad. For *you*," I said.

My mother laughed. "It's not working."

Jonathan's voice grew louder. "That's not how you calm people down! Lavender doesn't calm people down!"

"He may have a point there," my mother said.

Jonathan grew more frustrated.

"Mother, have a seat. You must be exhausted. Can I get you some wine?"

"I'm into that," she answered. "I just love that candle you have going in the bathroom. Summer Sweat."

"You mean Summer *Sweet*."

"That's weird. I thought it smelled like sweat," my mother said.

Jonathan turned to her. "And you *loved* it?"

I walked to the kitchen to pour some wine.

Jonathon picked up the remote and turned to the local news channel. "There he is. My opponent."

My mother climbed into the macrame hammock. "What's that dude's name again?"

"Congressman Malcolm Hyde."

Malcolm Hyde was a sixty-year-old bureaucrat who spent his entire adult life in government. He combed his dyed black hair straight back and pasted it down with an excessive amount of gel. He had a handlebar mustache and a lengthy goatee. He gelled the ends of his handlebar mustache and twisted the tips upward with his fingers when he spoke.

My mother shook her head at the TV. "Who would vote for him?"

"So far, just about everybody," Jonathan said. "He's way up in the polls."

I approached them with a glass of wine for my mother and a cup of coffee for Jonathan. After serving both, I snuggled next to Jonathan on the sofa.

"Hyde's up in the polls for now," I said, "but Jonathan's gaining ground fast. Knowing Hyde's knack for dirty tactics, this could get ugly."

I continued to snuggle and flirt with Jonathan, despite my mother's presence. She'll have to get used to it. "I can't wait to be a married couple," I whispered to him.

Apparently, my words were loud enough for her to hear. She sighed. "I don't know why people think they need government's approval to validate their relationship. Why not just live together?"

"Being married is a beautiful commitment," I answered.

My mother scoffed at the idea. Then she tilted her head, studying our flirtatious behavior. "As a couple, I have to admit that you two have a totally awesome aura. It's like you were made for each other."

"How so?" I asked.

"Haven't you seen those couples who've been together for decades? After a while, they begin to look alike. I already see similar traits you two have in common."

Jonathan did a double-take at my mother. "You think we look alike?"

"No. Not really," she answered. "But in the short time I've been with you today, I see little facial expressions that you're picking up from each other. Things like that."

That made me laugh. "We only met a couple of months ago. I think you're imagining that."

"Maybe so. Anyway, it blows my mind to think that in two days, I'll be seeing Cousin Cosmo and the rest of the tribe."

I dug into Jonathan's arm. "Sorry, Mother. I'm afraid we didn't invite him."

"What? And why not?"

"Well, he wears a cape."

"So what?"

I glanced at Jonathan. "It'll make Jonathan's relatives uncomfortable."

She sat up straighter. "It's his trademark. He's always worn that cape. In some circles, they consider that stylish."

"Nineteenth-century London?" Jonathan asked.

My mother chugged half her wine. "So, you're both embarrassed by Cosmo and his cape."

I tried to explain in a sympathetic tone. "We just decided that, well, with this campaign and all, there might be some press there. Maybe a few photographers. We're trying to be careful about appearances. About everything. Do you understand?"

"No. I don't. What about Tanya? You grew up with her. She'll be there, right?"

I quickly refilled my mother's wine glass. "I'm afraid we didn't invite Tanya, either."

"Piper! I can't believe this! Tanya doesn't even own a cape."

"Mother, it's not that."

"Then what is it?"

I raised both eyebrows at Jonathan as encouragement for him to jump in. But he held his hand out, palm up, prompting me to answer.

I paused. Then stated the reason. "Tourette's."

"Bingo," added Jonathan.

"Piper, what does Tourette's syndrome have to do with anything?"

"During the speak-now-or-forever-hold-your-peace thing, I don't need her shouting out, 'Eff this effin' wedding!'"

"That's a headline we don't need," said Jonathan.

My mother shook her head in anger. "I think she got over that issue with Tourette's. She's fine now. She's cured. I can't believe you're excluding her from the guest list. Piper, this isn't like you."

I rose from the sofa and sat next to her in the hammock.

"I know, Mother. You'll just have to understand. I can't have any problems that day. Once we get past this wedding, we can loosen up."

She took a long, deep breath. "Fine. What about Uncle Arnold?"

"The term life insurance salesman?"

She reluctantly nodded. "Say no more."

"Mother, the guest list was getting too big. We had to make some tough decisions."

She stopped sipping her wine and stared out the window. "I'm afraid to ask about Florina."

I handed my mother the entire bottle of wine.

"Is that the gypsy psychic?" Jonathan asked.

She jerked her head in Jonathan's direction. "She's Romanian!"

I pleaded my case. "She carries a crystal ball—everywhere she goes."

My mother turned back toward me with puppy dog eyes. "But she's very discreet about it."

Jonathan wondered aloud. "Is that anything like a discreet wrecking ball?"

"Mother, do you remember the last family wedding we went to?"

"Florina had nothing to do with that."

Jonathan said, "I don't even want to know."

"No one remembers anyway," my mother insisted.

"*I* do," I said. "Florina set up her crystal ball at Tony's wedding reception. She predicted the exact day Tony's marriage would collapse—which was that very day!"

"Lucky guess," my mother said.

"Remember who showed up? Tony's furious current wife. Who knew?"

"Florina's crystal ball knew," Jonathan added.

I said, "Florina ruined that wedding with her psychic abilities."

My mother turned her nose up and closed her eyes. "Maybe too many wives ruined it." She opened her eyes and put her hand on mine. "I learned a valuable lesson that day."

"About infidelity?"

"What? No. I learned to never throw away a wedding gift receipt."

"Mother, I hope you understand. Jonathan and I talked about it, and he thinks a newspaper photo of our wedding reception featuring a crystal ball and a séance might not be helpful."

She pursed her lips and turned away from me.

The conversation ended, and we sat there in awkward silence.

CHAPTER 6

As we sat without speaking, something was gnawing at me. "Oh, God!" I checked my watch. "I completely forgot that I'm meeting Cassie for a drink on State Street."

"I'm not in the mood to do that," my mother said. "You go ahead. I just need to meditate and think about my family—those poor souls who won't get the chance to attend one of the rare family weddings that come along. Don't worry about me. I'll just stay here and stare blankly out the window at nothing."

"That's fine. Jonathan can stare out the window with you. Let him know if you spot any Girl Scouts doubling as spies."

My mother furrowed her brow at my comment. "What?"

I grabbed my car keys off the counter and hurried to the door. "Jonathan will explain. I'll be right back."

Jonathan rose from the sofa. "I need to head home. There are a few things I need to catch up on."

"Mother, will you be okay here alone?"

She waved her hand at me. "I've been alone all my life. I think I can handle an hour or two more. Besides, a candlelit bath with plenty of lavender will calm my aura."

We reached the upscale bar and grill on the palm tree-lined street in downtown Santa Barbara just as dusk fell. The Crow's Nest is a small lounge located among Mediterranean and Spanish-style shops with stark white exteriors and red tile roofs.

CHAPTER 6

The interior was dark. I needed a minute for my eyes to adjust to the lack of light. I finally spotted Cassie in a booth along the far wall.

As I approached her, Cassie motioned with her head at the man sitting in the booth behind me. He was middle-aged with a thick body. He had an unshaven face that featured deep-set eyes that darted about. His curly black hair leaked out from the bottom edge of a blue Dodger ball cap, and his sideburns were wiry and untrimmed.

Cassie signaled with her hand for us to keep our voices low so that he couldn't eavesdrop on our conversation.

I hugged her before I sat down. "Have you been here long?"

"Fifteen minutes. I was beginning to wonder if you forgot."

"Almost. I was in the middle of breaking the news to my mother that we wouldn't be inviting most of our oddball relatives to the wedding. We tried to downsize the guest list anyway, but mostly it's Jonathan who's paranoid that it'll be a freak show."

"How would he know that? He's never met them. For that matter, he barely just met *you*."

"Unfortunately, I told him the crazy stories of all the incidents at family gatherings through the years."

"And how did Harmony take the news?"

"Not well. She's soaking in a lavender bath and calming her aura."

"Awww. Poor thing."

A server approached our table, and we both ordered a cocktail.

I said, "Thanks for meeting me. I needed a break. Trying to hold everything together is taking its toll on me. Jonathan seems to be hanging in there. He'd normally be fine, but dealing with his sleazy opponent is making him distrustful about everyone and everything."

The front door of the bar and grill opened. An older man with slick-backed hair entered while stroking his black mustache with one hand and carrying a large envelope in the other.

"Cassie," I whispered. "That's Congressman Malcom Hyde. Oh,

God. He's coming our way!"

The Congressman sat in the booth behind me. So close that if I leaned back, our heads would touch. Cassie and I stopped talking and listened.

"I'm Hyde. You Griggs?"

The man in the Dodger cap answered, "The one and only."

"Good. I like your confidence. I hope you can back it up with results. They tell me you're the top private eye in town."

"I ain't gonna argue with that," Griggs said.

Facing the opposite direction prevented me from seeing either man, but Cassie was staring at them with wide-open eyes. Too wide open.

"Cassie," I mouthed. "You look like you saw a ghost."

Cassie took a deep breath and tried to relax.

The envelope Hyde carried in his hand hit the tabletop with a *plop,* followed by the rustling of papers.

"Griggs, as you can see by our internal polling data, the gap between me and my opponent, Jonathan Knight, is closing. That's a trend that needs to stop. And it needs to stop now. I have too much going for me here to lose it all to some rookie full of noble ideals and stars in his eyes."

Griggs didn't respond, and I assumed he was perusing the data.

Hyde continued. "This is Knight's one-sheet flyer."

"Is this a photo of Jonathan Knight?" Griggs asked.

"Yep, that's the idiot alright."

Cassie's eyes narrowed and her lips pursed. She started to stand, but I reached out and held her wrist. I shook my head, and she sat back down.

Hyde scoffed. "I received that flyer in the mail yesterday. Look at that nonsense. A vote for Jonathan is a vote for common sense."

I proudly mouthed, "*I* thought of that slogan."

Hyde added, "What total imbecile came up with that?"

I clenched my fist and tried to scoot out of the booth, but Cassie held on to my arm, stopping me.

Hyde said, "Here's what I want you to do. Tattoo Mr. Goody-two-shoes' face to your brain."

"No need. I'll just remember it," said Griggs.

"It's an expression, you idiot."

Griggs fake-laughed. "Yeah. Yeah, I know that."

"You listen to me, Griggs. I want you to stick like glue to that jackass. Everybody's got a skeleton in their closet. Your job is to find some dirt or something useful and bring it back to me. I have the press in my back pocket. Anything I give them will be front-page news, I guarantee you."

Griggs cleared a case of nerves from his throat. "Yeah, but what if he don't got nothin'. Sometimes, people are as clean as a whistle."

The booth shook and someone scooted across the vinyl seat. Cassie gathered the top of her blouse in her fist to convey to me that Hyde had a fistful of Grigg's shirt.

Hyde said in an angry, gravelly, deliberate voice, "Don't tell me some people have nothing to hide. There's no such thing. Your job is to find it. Now, can you handle this assignment, or should I get someone else?"

Griggs's voice filled with fear. "You ain't got no worries. I'm on the case. I'll bust that character doing somethin', you'll see."

"That's the attitude I want to see. Now, listen up. He's marrying some airhead—a rookie attorney. She works in the public defender's office." They both let out a hearty laugh.

My jaw clenched. As I turned to slide out of the booth, Cassie reached across the table and held on to me again.

"Griggs, see what you can dig up on her. Hang around her house too. Dig through their trash cans. Oh, and the wedding rehearsal would be a good place to do some sniffing around."

Griggs mumbled over the sound of scribbling. "Wedding rehearsal. Got it."

"So, come up with something I can go to the press with. If you don't, you won't work in this town again. Got it?"

"Got it."

"Let's meet back here at the same time tomorrow. I want to see what you've come up with."

A cocktail waitress approached their booth as the men scooted out.

"You took too long," Hyde said to her.

As they headed toward the front door, she glared at them.

"You've got to tell Jonathan right away," Cassie said.

I shook my head. "No. He's paranoid enough. This will send him over the edge."

"Then what are you going to do?"

"Jonathan is squeaky clean. He's got nothing to hide. And now that my crazy distant relatives won't be at the wedding, I have nothing to worry about either. I think the best thing is to keep this to ourselves."

CHAPTER 7

The next day, Jonathan's father planned to treat the wedding party to lunch at a pricey restaurant. He and my mother had never met, and he wanted to get that out of the way before the rehearsal dinner later that night.

While I sat at the kitchen table in front of my laptop, my mother came out of my guest room with her purse, a faded sundress, and flip-flops.

"Mother, Jonathan's father made reservations at a very expensive restaurant. Is that what you're wearing?"

"I have other plans. And this attire will be perfectly acceptable where I'm going."

I stood in front of the door and held up my hand to stop her. "You *have* to go! It's not a choice. The reason for the lunch was for you to meet Jonathan's father before the rehearsal dinner."

She waved off the entire idea. "I've heard all about him and from what they tell me, I won't be missing much."

"Please don't do this."

"Piper, you yourself said he's an uptight grump. Why do I need to deal with that?"

I rubbed my temple, preparing for the headache that was sure to come. "Mother, I don't think I used those words. I think I said he's meticulous and very serious. That's a far cry from uptight and grumpy."

She laughed. "Meticulous and serious isn't floatin' my boat, either."

"What other plans could you possibly have? You don't know a

soul around here."

"I have an appointment at the New Age Spa. While you're dealing with grumpy pants, I'll be exfoliating and wearing a raw honey mask while enjoying the sounds of the forest."

"Is there anything I can say or do to talk you into joining us for lunch?"

"Nope. Sorry, but from the stories I've heard, Jonathan's father has a vibe I don't dig."

I moved aside and let her pass by.

As she passed, she pinched my cheek. "Love ya, Piper. See you tonight."

Cassie and I took my car to downtown Santa Barbara. We met Jonathan and Howie in the restaurant's waiting area near the hostess' station.

"Hi, Howie," Cassie said with a huge grin.

Howie's eyes widened. "Cassie, you look beautiful."

She wore a light green V-neck summer dress, and I chose a deep red vintage ruffle blouse with three-quarter sleeves and a black pencil skirt.

Jonathan approached me and kissed me before I had a chance to say hello.

"I still can't believe I'll be the lucky guy married to you," he said. "You look amazing."

"This ol' thing?" is what I said about the outfit that took two and a half hours to put together. I flashed a flirty smile and said, "I almost forgot what I wore."

The hostess approached us. "Walter Knight, your table is ready."

"Thank you," Jonathan said to her. "We're part of Walter's party, but he isn't here yet. When he arrives, will you show him where we're seated?"

"Surely."

We followed her into the dining area, where she seated us at a large, round table.

CHAPTER 7

Howie fidgeted in his seat as he surveyed the surroundings. Polished leather chairs and cozy mahogany tables filled a room with adobe-like walls, an enormous fireplace, and an open beam ceiling. Howie lowered his voice, but not enough to keep it from my ears. "I hope your dad is picking up the tab. I would've been just fine at The Waffle House."

Jonathan said, "Well, this place was his idea, so maybe he will."

"What do you mean, *maybe*? Is there a chance he won't?"

"Howie, just relax. Everything will be fine."

"But what I order depends on who's paying."

Jonathan leaned toward me. "Where's Harmony?"

"She had a new age spa appointment. She's not coming."

Jonathan rested his forehead on his fingers. "This entire idea was my dad's so he could meet her."

"I tried my best. I really did. But she already made her mind up."

"Well, guys, it's finally here," Howie said. "The wedding rehearsal is tonight. Nervous?"

"I'm not nervous until somebody asks me if I'm nervous. That's when I get nervous," Jonathan said.

To Jonathan, Cassie said, "I'm excited to get to know your father."

"That's because you've never met him," Jonathan said.

"Why do you say that? What's he like?"

Jonathan picked up his glass of water and sipped it. "Well, my father is a no-nonsense businessman, will always be a no-nonsense businessman, and will most likely die a no-nonsense businessman. He'll never have one of those deathbed regrets of spending too much time at the office." Jonathan signaled for a server to take their drink orders.

After we ordered our drinks, Cassie asked, "Was he always like that? Obsessed with business?"

"As far as I can remember. He's just a serious man. Nose to the grindstone. All he wanted to do was manage his business. A career change to something like stand-up comedy was never in the cards for him."

Cassie covered her mouth to hide her laugh.

As soon as the words left Jonathan's mouth, his father followed the hostess into the dining room. Walter Knight wore a permanent expression of seriousness on his face—probably since childhood, I'm guessing. Jonathan said he can remember his dad smiling a few times through the years but couldn't recall him laughing outright. As miserable a curmudgeon as he was, he was handsome. He had graying hair and an unexplainable tan. The only way this workaholic got a tan was from an overly intense desk lamp.

Jonathan stood to hug his dad, but Walter headed that off with a handshake.

A nod of the head while saying *Son* was Walter's warm and fuzzy way of greeting Jonathan.

Walter also offered Howie a curt nod. "Howard."

"Dad, it's *Howie*. Only his mother and probably his urologist call him *Howard*."

Howie glanced at Cassie to see if she'd heard that remark, but she was saying something to me and missed it altogether. Howie breathed a sigh of relief.

"Dad, this is Cassie. The maid of honor."

"Glad to meet you, young lady."

Walter stepped over to me and hugged me. I was pleasantly surprised to get a hug.

Asking Walter a question made me nervous, but I took a deep breath and asked anyway. "Would you mind if, after the wedding, I call you *Dad*?"

He paused before his answer, studying my face. "Sure. If you wish."

I hugged him again.

"Piper, is your mother in the restroom?" Walter asked, while looking around.

"I'm afraid she couldn't make it. She had an appointment she couldn't get out of."

Walter's brow furrowed, and his eyebrows pulled together.

"She was a big part of why we planned this lunch."

"I know. She did her best to get here. The good news is, she'll meet you tonight at the rehearsal dinner."

"I suppose," he said, scanning his menu.

After we ordered our food, Walter said, "Son, I've been too damn busy with my business lately. I wanted to take some time and catch up on all that's going on. I feel bad that I haven't been able to be very involved. Is everything running smoothly?"

"So far, Dad. But it'll be a big relief to get past this and back to normal."

Walter said, "I have all the info at the office. I'll have my assistant text me the address of the church."

Jonathan turned to me and waited for me to respond.

Time to swallow hard again. "The wedding's at the beach."

"Okay. So the church is at the beach. Which church? I need the address."

"Dad, Piper wanted a romantic beach wedding. There's no church."

Walter frowned. "A beach wedding?"

"*On* the sand," Howie added.

Jonathan waved Howie off. "You're not helping."

"They'll be barefoot. It's cute," Cassie added.

Walter turned to his son. "You won't be wearing dress shoes at your wedding?"

"Neither of us will," I said.

"Oh, I'm wearing shoes. You can count on that, dad."

Walter grew more disturbed by the second. "No church? No minister? Not even a priest?"

"Piper's mother found a guy to do the officiating."

"Online," Howie said.

Jonathan turned away from his dad and directed his gaze at Howie. Under his breath, Jonathan said, "Why did I bring you with me?"

"This minister is an online guy?" Walter asked.

"Yep. Afraid so," Jonathan replied.

"What religion?"

Howie jumped in again. "The Church of Planetary Unification."

Howie grimaced because Jonathan kicked him under the table.

Howie was always well-meaning, but he had a knack for throwing a wrench into the works. Jonathan once told me that Howie's parents threw a birthday party for their oldest teenage daughter. In front of everyone, Howie gave her a pillow as a gift. When she asked why a pillow, he explained he overheard her whisper on the phone that the backseat of her boyfriend's car was killing her back.

So, thanks to Howie, Walter now knew that the minister was from the Church of Planetary Unification.

Jonathan said, "Scheduling the minister was Piper's job. But she asked her mother to help with finding someone. Her mother found this minister." Jonathan was attempting to salvage something from a flaky scenario. "Dad, the reason this minister was selected was he'll accept Piper's credit card, giving her the points she'll apply toward our honeymoon costs. It's really all very sensible when you think about it."

"It'll be a beautiful service," I said.

Walter stared in silence.

Jonathan continued. "I've met him. He looks like any other minister. No one will think he's not."

"Except for the galaxy logo on his hat," Howie said.

Walter closed his eyes and shook his head. "Son, your mother is now rolling over in her grave."

Jonathan glared at Howie. Howie ran his thumb and index finger across his own lips as if he were zipping them together.

Our meals were served, and I hoped the great food would make the atmosphere less tense, but it didn't. We did our best to carry on while Walter complained about every little detail he learned of our wedding day plans. We all caught on—except Howie—that mentioning anything more about the wedding was tantamount to poking an ogre with a stick.

We were just finishing up our meals—in mostly awkward

silence—when Walter cleared his throat. "Son, do I need to remind you that Congressman Hyde is watching your every move? He's ready to pounce on any slip-up. This beachcomber wedding is problematic." He turned his attention to Howie. "And you. You're supposed to be his campaign manager. I'd suggest you start managing."

Then Howie stepped in it again. He said, "If you think the beach wedding is a problem, wait till Congressman Hyde finds out about the naked strangler—"

"Howie!" I shouted.

Cassie put her hand on Howie as a message to quit interjecting.

"The naked what?" Walter asked.

"It's nothing, really. Not a big deal," Jonathan said, glaring at Howie.

Walter groaned. "Do I even want to hear what a naked strangler has to do with the wedding?"

Howie answered by shaking his head.

Jonathan took a deep breath. "Let me explain. And Howie, feel free to blurt out anything I might have missed." Jonathan faced his father. "In this country, you're assumed innocent until proven guilty, right?"

"I'm listening."

"And if you can't afford an attorney, one will be appointed, right?"

"That's our system," Walter replied. "But what does that have to do with you?"

"Since Piper works in the public defender's office, they assigned her to defend… how do I say this…?"

"The naked strangler," Howie said.

Walter held his hand on his chest. "This is getting worse by the minute!"

"Is it your heart? Should we call an ambulance?" I asked.

Howie's eyes widened at the bill. "Get his wallet first."

Jonathan flashed a look of annoyance at Howie.

Howie was quick to clarify. "Just so no one at the hospital

steals it, is what I mean."

"C'mon, Dad. You're going to be fine."

In the middle of the chaos, Cassie nudged me and nodded to a corner of the restaurant. Private investigator Griggs's blue Dodger hat was visible as he peeked through a leafy plant, snapping photos of our lunch with Walter.

CHAPTER 8

My mother, Cassie, and I were back at my condo, getting ready for the wedding rehearsal later that night. We were in my bedroom, organizing my things to prepare for the move to Jonathan's house in Montecito. I placed keepsakes and photo albums in a large cardboard box.

On my nightstand was a framed photo of Jonathan and me at the coffee shop from the days we first met, which was only two months earlier. I was seated at a small table in the corner when he first noticed me. Later, he confessed he fell instantly in love. I can admit now that I fell in love, too.

I remember that day in the coffee shop like it was yesterday. Jonathan said I had a distressed look on my face, and it caught his attention. I was mumbling at my laptop screen while reviewing a case about to come up for trial. He apologized for being presumptive and asked if I might need some help. As fate would have it, he was also a lawyer and used his seven years of legal experience to guide my case strategy in an effective direction.

After that, we happened to show up at the same time each morning. Was that just a coincidence? Eventually, the conversation shifted from legal jargon to discussing shared interests in books, movies, vacations, and future aspirations.

We went from talking in a coffee shop to walking on the sidewalk, then to the plaza, and eventually to a bench in the park. The time of the "coincidental" meetings changed from exclusively mornings to include lunchtimes, afternoons, and every evening on days that ended in y.

It truly was love at first sight. I wanted to say those three heart-stopping words, *I love you*, but my better judgment told me to wait. At least a few more days. Or maybe a few weeks before telling him—if I had the patience. Our expressions of affection to each other progressed through the usual declarations: *you're nice, I like you, you're fun, I adore you, I need you*, to finally, *I love you*. But *I love you* could easily have been the first assertion. It had become clear from the start that life would make no sense without each other. So, I found myself hiring an airplane that pulled a banner proposing something of great importance.

Cassie nudged my arm. "Hello? Piper. Are you still with us?"

Cassie's voice brought me back to the present.

"Sorry, I guess I was daydreaming."

My mother laughed. "You were trippin'."

I resumed the task of placing memorabilia into the box. "I was just thinking back to how Jonathan and I met. It was so romantic."

Cassie shook her head and smirked. "Oh, please. You're not going to tell your *how-we-met* story again, are you?" Cassie turned toward my mother. "Every time I hear it, I expect her to add a glass slipper to the story."

"I can do that," I joked.

"We missed you at lunch, Mother."

"How did it go?" she asked.

I glanced at Cassie. "Go ahead, Cass. Tell her."

Cassie's eyes widened. "It went okay, I guess. We're still alive."

My mother chuckled. "He's that bad, huh?"

"Well, he was sure interested in the wedding details. He couldn't stop talking about the beach," I said.

My mother said, "I'm glad I went to the New Age Spa. I'm relaxed and ready for tonight."

Cassie wanted to change the subject. "Harmony, how did you and Piper's father meet? And was it her father who encouraged her to become a lawyer?"

"Biological father," I clarified. "I only met him once. And he was a man of few words."

"No words of wisdom?"

"He was a mime," I said.

My mother wagged her finger at me. "Uh, excuse me. He was an actor. Classically trained."

"Mother, you told me he was a street performer. A juggler."

Cassie made a sad face. "The relationship didn't last?"

"Sadly, no," explained my mother. "A career and a family were the only things the dude couldn't juggle."

Cassie placed her hand on my mother's shoulder. "Awww. I'm sorry. It's not your fault. You tried."

"Oh, I tried a lot. Shacked up three more times after that, but I decided that a steady relationship gig wasn't in the stars for me."

"Love is not for everyone," I said.

My mother smiled and had a faraway look in her eye. "I was in love once. It was about the same time I met the juggler, but that other boy got away too, and the rest is history."

Ding dong!

I jumped up and hurried to the front door.

It was my neighbor Sherman.

"Hey, come in. What's up?"

Sherman was about the same age as me. He was a skinny man with thick eyeglasses. His clothes must have been straight off the rack from either Nerds R Us or GeekMart.

"Is this a good time?" he asked.

"Yeah, sure."

My mother left the bedroom and approached Sherman and me.

"Mother, this is Sherman. He lives next door. Sherman, this is Harmony."

She rushed over and hugged him, causing the poor guy to flail his arms as he was knocked off stride. After she allowed Sherman to pry himself loose, she asked, "So, you live next door with your wife and kids?"

"I wish," Sherman said. "I don't even have a girlfriend yet."

My mother hugged him again, turned her head toward me, and said, "Why do I have the urge to take this boy under my wings and mother him? He's just adorable!" She pinched his cheek and escorted him toward the living room.

Sherman took a few steps and stopped. "Do I smell sweat?"

I threw my hands up. His comment brought out the sarcasm in me. "Yeah, it's sweat. I have a candle burning called Summer Sweat. I thought it would be a *great* idea."

"It's just a lavender candle," my mother explained.

Sherman nodded. "It's strangely calming."

As we walked, Sherman tripped on a throw rug and went sprawling to the floor. His eyeglasses flew off and skidded across the room.

"Sherman!" my mother shouted as she rushed to his side.

I hurried over and kneeled beside him. Cassie retrieved his glasses.

He rolled over and grimaced. "I'm okay."

My mother stooped over him, close to his face. She cradled his head in her arms. "Are you sure? Sherman, can you hear us? Blink if you can."

I rolled my eyes. "He already said he's okay."

While cradling Sherman's head, she rocked back and forth, weeping silently.

"Mother, are you crying?"

She nodded. Her tears rained down on Sherman's face, and he wiped them with his sleeve.

"I don't know what's gotten into me," she said. "I really don't. I feel a connection to him like he's the son I never had. The son I always wanted. The child that would finally fulfill me as a mother."

"Thanks a lot," I said.

My mother moved her face even closer to Sherman and said, "Blink once, for *I'm okay*."

I added, "Or twice for *get her away from me*."

Cassie reached for Sherman's hand and pulled him to his feet. "Maybe you'd like to sit on the sofa for a minute."

Sherman sat up. "I'm all right. Really. This happens all the time. I'm a little klutzy anyway, and the fact that my eyesight is terrible doesn't help."

My mother held his arm and guided him to the sofa. "Somebody get him a glass of water. Hurry! He needs a glass of water!" As they sat on the sofa, she gently took the eyeglasses from Cassie's hand, placed them on Sherman's face, and continued to check him for injuries.

He said, "I didn't mean to interrupt anything. Piper asked me to stop by to pick up a few things to take to the wedding rehearsal."

My mother said, "You're not picking up anything 'til I know you're okay."

"I'll be fine." Sherman thanked her while looking at my mother with the facial expression of a wounded soldier on some imaginary battlefield.

"Tell me about yourself, Sherman," my mother said. "What do you do for a living?"

"I work at a forensic lab. Piper has hired us to do some work for her new case."

I interrupted. "We don't need to go into that."

My mother said, "I guess Piper's innocent client left his DNA all over town."

"*Alleged* DNA. I'm having it tested," I said.

"This is exciting," my mother said. "Like a TV show! What an awesome way to clear The Naked Strangler from wrongdoing. If you ask me, I think he's innocent."

Cassie asked, "Innocent of what? Being naked or strangling?"

My mother scoffed. "Strangling, of course. Naked is not a crime. If it were, I'd be doing twenty-five to life."

Cassie handed a glass of water to Sherman. "I'm not sure why you need this, but here you go."

The conversation might have been getting too weird for Sherman, so he said, "I better get those boxes and get on my way."

"Thank you, Sherman," I said. "They're in the guest room.

Only grab the boxes marked *rehearsal*."

Sherman stood up, and my mother also rose to her feet.

He didn't need help, but she steadied him with her hand, anyway. "Are you sure you can handle this? It's a big job carrying those boxes."

"He's got this, Mother."

She asked him again. "Are you sure?"

"Mother, he's almost thirty."

"Twenty-eight," Sherman said as he headed to the guest room to grab the boxes.

My mother studied him and muttered, "He's something. He's really something."

Sherman returned to the living room carrying two large boxes, one on top of the other.

I held up my hand. "Stop. I said only the boxes marked *rehearsal*."

Sherman angled his head to one side to read the markings. "I know. They're both marked *rehearsal*."

"Look again. One is labeled *receipts*."

"Oops. You're right." Sherman placed the top box on the floor and headed back to the guest room to return the bottom box."

I stopped him again. "Sherman. You're returning the wrong box."

My mother picked up the box of receipts and returned it to the guest room. When she approached Sherman with another box marked *rehearsal*, she said, "You take care, sweetie."

"Nice meeting you, Harmony. I'll see you all tonight at the rehearsal." He turned toward the door.

I really didn't want to be the one to tell him, but I did anyway. "That's the closet."

Sherman laughed at himself and left through the front door.

"I just love that boy," my mother said.

An hour had passed since Sherman left, leaving Cassie and I with just enough time to get to the Crow's Nest. Hyde and Griggs were meeting there again, and I had to see what scandalous info Griggs had promised to deliver.

My mother wanted to come with us, but she's not cut out for undercover work. So I told her we were headed to Woody's Burger Joint to satisfy our craving for greasy French fries. Being the earth momma she is, she changed her mind and said she'd rather walk across the street and grab a wheatgrass shake.

We dashed out the door and were soon speeding down State Street. Behind the Crow's Nest was a small parking lot, perfect for discreet parking. But being new at sleuthing, we didn't know any better and instead parked on the street right in front of the bar.

Wearing wide brim hats and large sunglasses, we entered through the front door and scanned the booths for Hyde and Griggs. They were nowhere in sight.

"They're not here. Let's go back to your place," Cassie said.

"We're a few minutes early. C'mon, let's grab a booth."

We chose the same booth we had last time.

The cocktail waitress approached us. "Can I get you movie stars a drink?"

I angled my head to see her face. "Movie stars?"

Cassie said, "The hat and glasses."

I nodded. "Oh. Right. Movie stars. I get it."

The waitress feigned a laugh.

I did some quick thinking and pointed to the sunglasses and the wide brim hats. "UV protection. Can't be too careful, you know."

The waitress stared at me. "We're indoors."

Cassie said, "Doesn't matter these days. That ozone layer is completely gone."

The waitress cocked her head to one side and pointed to our arms. "But you're both in short sleeves."

I glanced at Cassie, snapped my fingers, and said, "I knew we forgot something."

"I'll have a glass of wine," Cassie said to the waitress, changing the subject.

"Me too."

The waitress raised both brows and walked away.

As soon as the server was far enough away, Cassie said, "I told you we should've taken the glasses off. We look like idiots."

"Better to look like idiots than be recognized."

Cassie checked her watch. "We're out of time. We need to get to the rehearsal dinner."

"Let's stay a few more minutes."

The front door opened, and Griggs entered. He began walking our way.

"Look down," I said to Cassie. "And look away."

Griggs walked by our booth and sat three booths away.

"Oh, just great. We'll never hear them," I said.

The front door opened again, and Malcom Hyde entered. He stood still for a moment and scanned the bar. When he spotted Griggs, he nodded. He slowed when he passed our booth and stared at us. My heart raced. Luckily, he kept walking and stopped at Griggs' booth. "Let's move to another booth," Hyde said.

Cassie formed a victorious fist. "They might move closer to us."

Griggs slid out of the booth, and they moved to another booth, even farther away.

"What are we going to do now?" I asked.

"Follow my lead," Cassie said. She slid out of the booth and walked their way.

"Cassie!" I whispered. "What are you doing?"

She deepened her voice and spoke loud enough for them to hear. "We're right under the air-conditioning vent. I can't take the cold on my neck."

I don't know why she disguised her voice. They've never heard her speak until now. And her fake voice was way too low.

Cassie sat in the booth next to them. Once I sat down, she used her creepy, low voice and said, "Okay, that's better. Isn't this better, Ariel?"

I nodded. Then I whispered, "Ariel?"

CHAPTER 8

Cassie leaned forward and whispered, "I just watched The Little Mermaid for the fourth time. I guess that name popped into my head."

Cassie had her back to their booth, and I was facing them.

Both men appeared annoyed that we moved next to them, especially Hyde.

The waitress returned with our glasses of wine. "Is the ozone layer better over here?"

We nodded in silence.

She moved to the next booth. "What can I get you two?"

Hyde shooed her away with his hand. "Not now. Go away." Then he faced Griggs. "Okay, let me see what you have."

With a look of accomplishment, Griggs placed a folder in front of Hyde.

"You're lucky you know me," Griggs said while sucking on a toothpick.

"Well done. Let me see what you have," Hyde said. While opening the folder, he added, "Spreading some dirt on this Jonathan character will help me get rid of this pest, once and for all."

Griggs smirked and nodded.

Hyde pulled several large photos out of the envelope and studied each one.

"All I see here is Jonathan eating at a restaurant. Wait. Here's one. Who's the guy holding his chest?"

Griggs smiled with confidence. "That's his father havin' chest pains."

Hyde's head tilted at the photo. "Did he die?"

"Naw. He's fine."

Hyde flipped the photos back onto the table. "Let me get this straight. As the leading private investigator in this town, what you dug up are photos of my opponent dining at a local restaurant and helping his dad during a medical issue."

The blood drained from Griggs' face. "Well, yeah."

Hyde stood up and leaned across his desk toward Griggs. "I need something to *hurt* my opponent, not help him, you jackass!

Get back out there and uncover something useful, or I'll have my friends at city hall yank your business license! Am I clear?"

Griggs nervously nodded and hurried out of the bar.

Cassie covered her mouth to hide her giggling.

We gulped our wine and paid the bill. We had a rehearsal to attend.

CHAPTER 9

The evening of the wedding rehearsal had finally arrived.

Jonathan and I were excited about rehearsing the ceremony at the Santa Barbara Oceanfront Hotel, a sprawling twenty-acre complex on the Pacific Ocean shoreline. The grounds featured palm trees, green lawns, swimming pools, and over five hundred guest rooms. An elegant open-air patio would serve as the venue for the rehearsal and dinner afterward. The patio's circular structure was about thirty yards across, with a thick white wall lining its perimeter. Arched openings in the walls provided a view of the ocean and manicured grounds.

Just above the horizon, the red-amber sun painted the underside of the scattered clouds with brilliant colors ranging from red to yellow. A warm glow from the fading sun flowed through the archways on the ocean side of the terrace. The cool ocean breeze played with the strings of white lights spanning the courtyard and made the candles on the dinner tables flicker.

Jonathan rarely cared about impressing others, but he splurged on the rehearsal site in case the media covered the event.

Although my toes wouldn't be sinking in the sand that night, holding the rehearsal on the hotel's elegant patio made sense. The beach often became windy and cold after sundown, so we compromised, holding the rehearsal at night on the hotel site. The wedding would take place the following day on the sunny beach.

As far as the overall planning was concerned, we kept

Jonathan's father in the dark. Any complaints he might lodge would come when the evening's events were already in progress.

We had reserved a block of twelve rooms for the wedding party on the hotel's seventh floor. Jonathan, my mother, Walter, and I each had our own separate rooms, although mine was a bridal suite.

My suite contained a furnished living room, a kitchenette, a separate bedroom, an enormous bathroom, and a balcony. I had a choice of a room with a view of the mountains to the north or the ocean to the south. I selected the ocean view, of course. My wedding dress hung from a hanger in an open closet.

I sat before a makeup mirror in the bathroom and applied eyeliner. Cassie stood in front of a larger mirror, brushing her hair.

"I'm a little nervous about this rehearsal," I said.

"Don't be. Everything is fine."

"That's easy for you to say. You don't have Harmony for a mother."

Cassie laughed. "Oh, c'mon. What could go wrong?"

What could go wrong? Well, I was about to list all that could go wrong, but that would take half the night. So, to the question of what could go wrong, I simply answered, "A lot."

Someone knocked on the door.

"I'll get it. You just relax," she said.

Cassie opened the door. "Harmony, we were just talking about you. In a good way, of course."

"Hi ya, sweetie. Is my daughter in here?"

"She is."

My mother stepped into the suite.

"I'm in the bathroom, Mother."

I refocused my eyes to see my mother behind me in my makeup mirror. She was wearing a paisley kaftan dress with clashing vibrant colors such as tangerine, turquoise, and purple. Her sandals matched a brown leather belt studded with shiny jewels. A necklace made of wooden beads and exotic stones supported a large yellow tassel at the bottom. On her head was a blue felt fedora with more tassels.

With my tongue planted in my cheek, I said, "I thought you would wear something unique tonight?"

My mother faced the large mirror. "It's just a rehearsal. I'm saving the flamboyant outfit for the wedding. I'll make sure it's an attention-getter." She leaned down and kissed me on the cheek. "You look beautiful, baby."

"Did you see my wedding dress?"

My mother walked to the closet and examined the white A-line style dress. "Well, it's traditional—if you're into that sort of thing."

"I'm marrying into a traditional family, and that dress will be perfect."

"Suit yourself. I'm not into *traditional*. And that's been a tradition of mine for years."

Cassie paused while passing by the bathroom doorway. "I like your outfit, Harmony. It's bold."

"Don't encourage her, Cass."

As she studied me, my mother's eyes became teary. She said, "My little Piper, you'll be all grown up and married by tomorrow afternoon."

"Newsflash, Mother. I'm already grown up."

She shook her head, almost in disbelief. "Finally. A woman from my side of the family will be married."

Her comment made me smile. "A family tree that forks. Interesting."

"Is Jonathan's family going to be here tonight?" she asked.

"Only his dad. Which reminds me. His dad's name is Walter. Not Wally. Try to remember that."

"They sure like formal names in that family. It makes sense, though. You told me Walter was uptight."

"I said he was *forthright*."

"Same thing."

"Mother, just do me a favor and behave yourself tonight. Not everyone is as free-spirited as you. You're always saying *live and let live*, so this is your chance to *live and let live*."

My mother removed her hat and primped her hair in the mirror. "*You're* marrying into that family, not me. I'll put up with ol' Walt, but I don't have to like him."

"It's Walter."

Cassie stepped into the bathroom. "Okay, Cinderella. Ready to go to your wedding rehearsal?"

I stood up, took one more look in the mirror, and turned toward the door. Over my shoulder, I asked, "Coming, Mother?"

"You go ahead. I'll be down in a minute. I have some touching up to do."

Leaving her alone with such a vast assortment of makeup was a scary thought for me. She's been known to get carried away, and it wasn't clear if the hotel stocked the power tools necessary to remove the amount of makeup she's been known to apply.

Cassie whispered to me, "I can stay with her and make sure she looks normal."

"You're the maid of honor, not a miracle worker." Before opening the door, I tried one more time. "You look fine, Mother. Please come with us."

"I'll be right there."

Cassie and I left the room.

We entered the courtyard. Jonathan was wearing a dark suit and looking as handsome as I've ever seen him. Howie was standing next to him.

As I walked toward him, he flashed his perfect, warm smile at the sight of me. He reminded me of a model in a men's clothing magazine, and I never wanted to turn the page. Every time I was around him, his eyes drew me in. They were many things, but they were mostly kind. He always told me he loved me, but he didn't need to. His eyes spoke for him. They looked at no other woman the way they looked at me. He put his arms out, and I entered his warm embrace. At first, we didn't say a word. We held each other as if no other soul was around. Any nervousness or anxiety we might have been feeling had melted away. There we stood, in each other's arms, and all was well.

Jonathan pulled back to look at me.

I gazed back into his eyes. "My handsome fiancé," I said. "This was one of the last times I'll get to say *fiancé*." It's such an elegant title. Or is it a description? Whatever it is, it's a powerful aphrodisiac when that word crosses a woman's lips. Then I had a thought. Someday, if a woman referred to Howie as her fiancé, would the word still retain its power? That thought made me laugh.

Cassie hugged Jonathan and Howie. Then she spotted a bridesmaid and hurried off to say hello.

Howie stepped over to me and cleared his throat.

"Yes?" I asked.

He kicked at the floor a few times and cleared his throat again. "I was wondering about something. Is there any way you could ask Cassie if she likes me?"

That question surprised me. "What? If she likes you? Are we in the sixth grade?"

Howie shrugged. "Sometimes it's hard to know how to approach women."

"Why don't you write her a note asking if she likes you? You can draw boxes for checking *yes* or *no*."

Howie searched his pockets for a pen.

Jonathan pushed Howie's upper arm. "She's joking. Do not write her a note."

"But I can do that," Howie said. "That's a viable idea."

"Don't. And *you're* managing *me*? That's a scary thought. So, what's this sudden interest in Cassie all about?"

"I don't run into that many single women. And besides, I think she might like me."

"And why do you think that?" Jonathan asked.

"She looked at me earlier. At the elevator."

I turned on the sarcasm. "Oh, well. Say no more. That's the sign. I'm surprised you're both not up in her room right now."

Howie's eyes widened. "Really?"

Jonathan shook his head. "Howie, she looked at you because

you're the best man, and she's the maid of honor. Not because she sees her future children in your eyes, you knucklehead."

Howie wasn't discouraged. "If she looks at me again, I'll know she likes me."

I laughed. "Maybe you can ask her at recess. If she looks at you from the swing set, that's even better than a look from the elevator."

Howie nudged Jonathan. "Here comes your dad."

Walter entered the patio and searched the crowd until he spotted Jonathan waving at him.

He approached and shook Jonathan's hand. "Son, how are you?"

Then he shook my hand. Wow. Mr. Warmth.

"Piper, you look very nice tonight," he said.

He turned and shook Howie's hand. "Good to see you, Howard."

Jonathan said to Howie, "Don't let Cassie hear that name. You might lose her *and* your future children."

Leaning toward Jonathan, Walter lowered his voice to keep me from hearing. "I don't know about this whole thing."

His comment made me turn away and pretend to scan the room.

"Know about what?" Jonathan asked. "This is a nice place."

"It's not a church. What would your mother think?"

"She'd think her son is happy and about to marry the woman he loves."

"Happiness," Walter said with a frown. "It's not all it's cracked up to be."

"Dad, just smile. Please."

Walter put his hand to his head as if he had a headache. "I'm glad your mother didn't have to go through this."

"Go through what?"

"First of all, this wedding rehearsal is on a helicopter pad."

"What? Dad, people dream of having a rehearsal dinner on this terrace."

"Second of all," Walter continued, "tomorrow you'll be getting married on a beach. Your mother would faint at the thought.'

"That's what Piper wanted. I want to make her happy. I'm sorry that the beach is a problem."

Walter shook his head. "It's a beach. There's not even a crying room."

"Why does there need to be a crying room?"

Howie interjected, "For the groom."

Jonathan turned to Howie. "Once again, not helpful."

Howie said, "Just joking. Hey, I'm going to take a look around. See if anyone from the press or Malcolm Hyde's office is snooping around."

"Good thinking," Jonathan said. "We can't be too careful."

CHAPTER 10

Jonathan and I made the rounds and greeted the bridesmaids and other guests. As soon as we'd said hello to every single person, we joined Howie and Walter near the appetizers.

Cassie headed our way, pulling a man behind her. She was giggling when she finally reached us. "This is Brother Larry," Cassie said.

Brother Larry was a nervous-looking man. Beads of sweat appeared on his forehead, and his eyes darted from me to Jonathan and back to me again. He wore a floor-length white robe and a small, three-pointed box-shaped biretta on his head.

Brother Larry attempted a smile. "I'm looking for..." He reached into his pocket, pulled out a wrinkled scrap of paper, and read, "...Harmony."

"She's still in my hotel bathroom," I said, "troweling on more makeup. She'll be down soon."

"I'm Jonathan, the groom, and this is the bride."

We both shook Brother Larry's hand.

"Could I make a small request, Brother Larry?" Jonathan asked.

"A request? You want me to sing a song?"

Jonathan pointed. "Your hat. It has a galaxy with planets on it."

Brother Larry removed his hat and examined the logo. "Oh, right."

Jonathan, in his most polite voice, asked, "Can you please turn your hat around so that the galaxy logo isn't visible?"

"I can do that," Brother Larry said as he turned his hat backward.

Walter scrutinized Brother Larry from head to toe. "Who the hell is this?"

Howie answered. "He's from the Church of..." Howie turned to Brother Larry. "What church is it again?"

"The Church of Planetary Unification," Brother Larry said.

Cassie nodded and snapped her fingers. "Oh, right! The guy Harmony found online."

Walter threw his hands up. "Oh, good Lord."

Brother Larry said, "I'll be marrying Jonathan and Pepper."

"It's Piper," Jonathan corrected.

Brother Larry leaned close to Jonanthan. "You met another woman?"

"No. You got her name wrong. It's Piper."

Brother Larry grimaced. "Remind me to change the paperwork."

Walter's face reflected his revulsion. He turned to Brother Larry and asked, "So, for some reason that I can't fathom, you think the planets should be united?"

Jonathan's shoulders slumped as he turned to Walter. "Dad, please. Some other time."

Brother Larry scratched his head. "I'm okay with that, I guess."

Walter shook his head. "You're just okay with that? You guess? It's your church's name, for crying out loud!"

Brother Larry said, "They never covered *that* in the meeting."

Walter asked, "What exactly does your cult mean by *unification*?"

"Here we go," Jonathan said.

Brother Larry's eyes darted back and forth. "It would be cool if the planets would unify. Maybe."

Walter turned to Jonathan. "This is the guy who's going to marry you?"

Jonathan held his hands up to calm Walter. "Okay, Dad, he answered your question. Let's move on."

"No, he didn't," Walter said as he turned to Brother Larry.

"Planetary unification? Do you mean unifying in spirit or physically? Because if you want the planets to join together in one location, it'll throw the whole universe out of balance. We'll all be doomed. Who would want that?"

"Uh, I'll have to get back to you on that. I'm new here," replied Brother Larry.

Jonathan cocked his head to one side. "Wait. Is this your first wedding?"

"It's my first anything. I just got approved last night. This is my first assignment."

Jonathan glared at me.

I tried my best not to laugh. "Don't look at *me*. You're the one who told my mother over the phone to find someone."

"That's before I met your mother in person. You should have known this was trouble."

"Honey, he's got a license to marry us. That's all I need," I said.

Jonathan turned to Brother Larry. "You have a license, right?"

"Yep. I took a twenty-five-minute course."

"Oh, great," Walter interrupted. "Twenty-five minutes to become an expert on the divine properties of the solar system. Sounds about right."

Brother Larry lowered his voice while leaning toward Jonathan. "Do you have the money?"

Jonathan pulled back. "Can we take care of this later?"

Brother Larry shook his head. "Payment must be upfront. Most of the twenty-five-minutes covered this subject."

Jonathan reached for his wallet. "Do you accept credit cards?"

"No."

"Checks?"

"No."

"Cash? You only take cash?"

"I was told we just changed our policy to cash only."

Jonathan appeared unprepared for that payment method. He turned toward me. "We have two problems here. One. He won't take a credit card. And two. There go your points toward the honeymoon."

"I got this, honey." I dialed my phone. "Sherman... Where are you?... Okay... Great, just in time." Then I said to Brother Larry, "Give us one second."

Sherman entered the rehearsal area through the hotel doors. As he walked, he stared at the envelope in his hand and bumped into a hotel employee. Cash flew everywhere, and bills blew across the pavers.

"Sorry. I didn't see him," Sherman said.

Howie, Cassie, Sherman, and Brother Larry scrambled to collect the money.

I chuckled at the sight of the four chasing the illusive bills while Jonathan glared at me.

The hotel's event planner approached Jonathan. "Sir, there's a gentleman wearing a cape claiming he was invited. What shall I tell him?"

My eyes widened. "Cousin Cosmo?"

"Yes, ma'am, that was the name he used."

Jonathan's shoulders drooped. "Are you serious?"

"Very serious, sir. Shall I show him in?"

Jonathan hesitated. Then asked, "Doesn't the hotel have a policy against wearing capes?"

"I believe our cape policy was deleted at the turn of the last century."

I tugged on Jonathan's sleeve. "Well, he's here. Might as well let him in."

"Very well." The event planner made a hand motion, and a hotel staffer opened the door."

Cousin Cosmo strolled past the four who were picking up dollar bills from the floor without noticing them. He held his head high in a dignified manner. His cape blew in the breeze, calling attention to itself. He had a long black mustache that covered his mouth. He wore a blue sash under his coat, leading some to believe he might be a foreign dignitary or a royal, but he was a retired postal worker from Pacoima. He recognized me and headed in my direction.

"I was told this was a dinner," Cousin Cosmo said.

"We'll eat right after the rehearsal," I replied.

Cousin Cosmo and his cape whirled in another direction and strolled away.

I offered a little wave of my hand. In a volume just loud enough for Jonathan, I mumbled, "Hi, Cosmo. How are you? Thanks for the congratulatory speech. Glad to see you, too."

"I thought we scratched him from the guest list," Jonathan said.

"So did I."

Cousin Cosmo found a table of appetizers and finger foods and proceeded to stuff several items into a pocket sewn into the cape's lining.

"So, the cape is for stashing freebies," Jonathan concluded.

I added, "Let's keep an eye on the party favors."

Walter returned with a drink in his hand. He lifted the glass and said, "Son, you're going to need one of these."

Guests of the bridesmaids and groomsmen entered the patio and offered us their best wishes. None wore a cape.

Brother Larry returned to Jonathan and me. "Shall we begin?"

I craned my neck around Jonathan, trying to find my mother. "She's still not here, but I guess we can start."

I gestured to Cassie and the other three bridesmaids that it was time to rehearse. Howie rounded up Jonathan's three groomsmen from the bar. After a few minutes, everyone but my mother was ready.

"Okay, people, listen up. I'm Brother Larry from the Church of Pl—"

Walter cleared his throat. "Just… skip over that."

That must have interrupted Brother Larry's train of thought, and he stared with a vacant expression at the group. "Now, where *was* I?"

Jonathan helped him out. "You introduced yourself."

"Oh, yes. As I said, I'm Brother Larry, and I'll officiate the wedding tomorrow. This rehearsal shouldn't take too long. We'll just walk through it." He pulled a small instruction booklet from his robe and read from it. "Okay, everyone should gather at the front of the church. From there, you'll proceed down the aisle." He lowered the booklet. "Oh. We're not in a church."

Walter frowned. "Don't remind me."

Brother Larry pointed at a spot on the patio about fifty feet away. "Everyone, just go over there. And I need someone to place a few chairs in a line right here to form an aisle." Then he consulted his booklet and read, "The groom, his best man, and his groomsmen shall be standing at the altar. Huh. Okay, there's no altar, so you guys just stand here by me, and we'll pretend there's an altar."

My bridesmaids and I gathered at the spot Brother Larry suggested.

Brother Larry shouted the rest of his instructions, allowing us to hear him from our distant position. "Now, everyone, please pretend you're in a church, I guess."

"The wedding is on the sand—at the beach—remember?" I shouted back to him.

"Right." He read the booklet again. "The bridesmaids are to proceed down the aisle." He flipped through a few pages. He lowered the booklet and shouted to the group, "It doesn't say how to determine which bridesmaid goes first. Okay, bridesmaids, let's do this—walk in the order of who has the closest relationship to the bride. Her favorite bridesmaid goes first."

I said, "No, no, no. Not a good idea."

Brother Larry asked me, "Should we go by weight?"

I ignored him and told the bridesmaids to walk in the order we all agreed on earlier—based on height.

I pulled my mobile phone out of my pocket and dialed my mother. "Mother. Where are you? We started… Okay, just hurry."

"Wait!" Brother Larry shouted while looking at his booklet. "The groom's father shall be the first to walk down the aisle."

Walter sat in a chair near the pretend altar. "I don't think I'll be walking down what will be a sandy aisle. I'll be seated in the front row already."

Brother Larry flipped back several pages and said, "Sorry, I got that wrong. The groom's father isn't the first to march down the aisle. But if you want to be seated already, I guess that's fine."

"Good," Walter said.

"Okay, let's have the first bridesmaid come down the aisle," Brother Larry shouted.

One bridesmaid proceeded with slow, deliberate steps.

"Hang on!" Brother Larry held his hand up. "You'll be walking in the sand. This is as good a time as any to practice shuffling your feet like you're trudging through that stuff. Like this." Brother Larry ran down to where the bridesmaids were standing to show what he wanted. He slid his feet forward, one at a time, without lifting his shoes off the pavers. As he trudged through the imaginary sand, he swung his arm and hunched forward from the weight of what he later described as an imaginary cooler full of imaginary drinks.

I interrupted. "I don't think that's necessary. I'd rather them walk normally."

Brother Larry shrugged. "Okay, but I was just trying to prepare them for walking on the sand."

The other bridesmaids followed and took their places on one side of the pretend altar.

Cassie was next. She wiped her teary eyes, hugged me, and walked down the aisle toward Brother Larry.

Brother Larry consulted his booklet again. "Okay! Flower girl! You're up!"

I shouted, "There's no flower girl."

Brother Larry didn't look up from his booklet. "No, it says here that the flower girl walks down the aisle at this time."

Losing patience, I shouted again. "Brother Larry, there's no flower girl."

"No problem. We'll just pretend there is one." He smiled at an imaginary flower girl walking toward him and whispered, "She's soooo adorable." He glanced up from the book. "Next up is the Bride's mother!"

I glanced around and checked my watch. My mother was late and nowhere to be seen. "She's on her way, but let's just move on."

"We can deal with that," Brother Larry said. He smiled and motioned with his hand to proceed.

"Who are you motioning to?" I asked.

"I'm pretending that your mother is walking toward me." He smiled as he pretended to watch the pretend mother of the bride walk down the aisle. Under his breath, he muttered, "Just look at her. What an elegant lady. An example of pure class."

Out of the side of his mouth, Jonathan whispered to Howie, "That answers my question. He's never met Harmony."

I wagged my finger at him from fifty feet away. I didn't have to hear his words to know he made a smartass remark.

"And here comes the bride," Brother Larry announced.

Despite being just a rehearsal, my heart raced as I practiced walking down the aisle.

Brother Larry mimicked what he guessed would be the wedding guests' reaction to my dress. "Ooooh. Awwww. Ooooh. Awwww. Stunning. Simply stunning."

I glanced at Jonathan and rolled my eyes.

As I reached Brother Larry, Jonathan stepped forward. He and I faced each other. I placed both my hands in his.

Beads of sweat appeared on Brother Larry's forehead. "Okay, great. We rehearsed the procession up the aisle. Now let's rehearse the vows. I'm going to cut right to the chase here. Jonathan, repeat after me. I Jonathan…"

"I Jonathan…"

Brother Larry smiled. "That went well."

"Please, go on," I said.

Brother Larry appeared to be thrown off track by my suggestion to continue. "Oh. Yes. Yes. Let's continue. Repeat after me, Jonathan. I Jonathan, take thee, Pepper…"

"Piper," Jonathan said.

"Oh, right. Take thee, Piper…"

My mother ran up the makeshift aisle toward the wedding party. "Wait! I'm here! What did I miss? Oh, you must be Brother Larry."

"Glad to meet you," Brother Larry responded. "Please, have a seat right there across the aisle from the groom's father."

My mother located her seat, but before she sat down, she spotted Sherman and latched onto him with an enormous hug. She turned toward the wedding party. "I just love this boy!"

"Please," Brother Larry insisted, "be seated."

My mother sat down and glanced across the pretend aisle at Walter. She was curious to see what Jonathan's father looked like. I expected to see her scowl upon seeing him, based on his reputation. But her eyebrows raised, and her lips formed a smile. I could be mistaken, but it appeared she added an approving nod. She faced Jonathan and me again, but her eyes continued to dart back at Walter. For a moment, she stared at the ground and appeared lost in her thoughts. She rubbed her chin and glanced at him again, but this time, her eyebrows raised as high as they could. "Wally?"

Jonathan's head and my head swung toward Walter.

Walter studied her face for a moment. Then his mouth fell open. "Chipmunk?"

CHAPTER 11

Upon hearing the name *Chipmunk*, our heads swung back toward my mother.

The wedding party gasped.

"Wait—wait—wait!" I said. "You two know each other?"

Jonathan's jaw dropped as he turned toward his father. "*Wally?*"

I faced my mother. "*Chipmunk?*"

My mother turned sideways in her chair toward Walter. "Wallypog, I can't believe it's you!"

"Wallypog?" asked Jonathan. "This is getting worse!"

My mother shrieked with joy, "I'm freaking out here!"

"That makes four of us," Jonathan said.

I turned to Jonathan. "What just happened?"

"Chipmunk," Walter said, "after all these years!"

"I think I'm having one of your mother's flashbacks," Jonathan said to me. "Is that even possible?"

Brother Larry frantically flipped through the pages of his booklet to see how to handle this particular scenario but found nothing.

While staring at Walter, my mother moved to the end chair on her side of the aisle, reducing the distance between them to about eight feet.

"Wally, I never thought I'd ever see you again!"

"Please, people. We're rehearsing the vows," Brother Larry pleaded.

"This is a trip!" my mother shouted. She took a long look at Walter and said, "I gotta say, Wally, you're still hot."

"No. My Dad's not allowed to be *hot*." Jonathan's head pivoted toward me for help.

My mouth was open, and I attempted to utter words, but nothing came out.

Jonathan turned back to Walter. "*Wally?* Seriously, Dad? Since when were you *Wally?*"

A smile formed on Walter's face. "It was a long time ago, Son. It was another lifetime ago. I was a different person then."

"Seems like only yesterday," my mother said. "Even as an older, more mature man, you're still handsome. A little grayer and maybe stockier, but it's still you, Wally."

"And you haven't changed a bit," Walter said. "Any man would admit that you're still a beautiful woman—*if* he could get beyond all that… that… that… bohemian garb you're still wearing."

Brother Larry slapped his palm against his forehead. "For God's sake. I'm trying to rehearse their vows here."

A waiter walked by with a tray of glasses and a bottle of wine.

"Waiter," Jonathan called out.

The waiter approached Jonathan. "Wine, sir?"

Jonathan took an empty glass off his tray. "Fill 'er up," he said. "And don't stop till you see it running down my sleeve."

Brother Larry frowned. "Drinking at this time during the vows is highly inappropriate."

My mother laughed. "Not even Florina's crystal ball could've predicted this!"

"Who's Florina?" Walter asked.

"Someone you'll never meet," said Jonathan.

Brother Larry was exasperated. "I'll just have a seat. Let me know when this family reunion is over." He sat on a nearby chair and waited for the server with the wine bottle to pass his way again.

The hotel's event planner stood across the room and waved his hand to get my attention. I wasn't sure he was waving at me, so I pointed at myself and mouthed the word *me?* The event planner nodded.

"Excuse me, Jonathan. He wants to tell me something."

Jonathan was still staring at his father and didn't answer.

I walked to where the event planner was standing. "Yes?"

"Dinner is ready to be served. How much longer will the rehearsal be?" he asked.

I hurried toward Brother Larry and asked, "Are we about done?"

A listless Brother Larry sat with his head resting on one hand. He waved once at the air with the other hand, signaling he had no hope of regaining control of the rehearsal.

I gave my permission to the event planner to serve dinner.

White linen tablecloths covered round tables and filled one side of the outdoor terrace. Each place setting had a card with a name on it. Jonathan, my mother, Walter, Cassie, Howie, and I sat at the head table. The bridesmaids, groomsmen, and others filled the remaining tables.

My mother grabbed the card with Howie's name written on it and switched it with hers so that she'd be next to Walter.

As we were seated, I said, "I'm in shock that you two know each other."

"Maybe it's fate," my mother said.

Jonathan shook his head. "No. It's not fate."

My curiosity was killing me. "So, what's the story?"

Jonathan closed his eyes. "There's no story. I'm sure there's no story."

A devious smile crossed my mother's lips. "Oh, there's a story, alright."

"Let's not talk about it," Jonathan said.

I shoved Jonathan in a playful way. "I want to hear this."

"C'mon, get to the story!" Cassie urged.

My mother said, "Wally, you go first."

Jonathan whispered to me that if he hears the name *Wally* one more time, he'll throw up.

Walter laughed a little and shook his head. "It was a long time ago—"

"Okay, it was long ago," Jonathan interrupted. "Lots of things happened a long time ago. We get it. How 'bout those Dodgers? Huh? They're only two games behind the Giants."

"Let him tell the story," Howie said.

Jonathan glared at Howie.

The hotel event planner approached Jonathan. "Sir, there's a woman here with a crystal ball. She says she's a guest."

My mother squealed with delight. "Florina!"

Walter nodded at Jonathan. "I guess I *am* going to meet Florina after all."

"Mother, what have you done? Cousin Cosmo and now Florina? I thought we made ourselves clear about the guest list."

She said, "Yes, you were very clear about the *wedding* guest list. This is the rehearsal. You said nothing about that, so I made a few calls."

"Just great," Jonathan said sarcastically.

There wasn't a chance Florina's entrance would go unnoticed. Her large and colorful flowing skirt matched her headscarf, and both shimmered with glitter as she hurried toward their table. Her multiple gold bracelets, necklaces, and earrings jingled like wind chimes. It was as if she couldn't decide which accessories to wear, so she wore them all. She guarded a glass sphere with one hand, holding it close to her body. With her free hand, she smothered us with hugs and sloppy kisses on our cheeks—except for Jonathan. He was the lucky beneficiary of a sloppy wet kiss planted squarely on his mouth. When she finally let go and allowed him to come up for air, he used his sleeve to wipe away the residue from the unsolicited and, I'm sure, unwanted kiss.

A waiter interrupted Florina's greeting and filled everyone's glass with champagne.

"What's that?" Howie asked, pointing at Florina's glass sphere.

Florina's eye's lowered to the spot Howie was pointing. "Oh, this? It's what I'm most known for in our family. You'll see." She leaned down and whispered into my mother's ear, "You should be very excited about what I saw in the ball today."

My mother's eyes lit up with a sparkle and she shook her body a few times, as if Florina's words had given her the chills.

"Okay, Florina," Jonathan said. "There's a seat next to Cosmo over there. Enjoy your meal, and we'll all talk later."

Florina had just received the brush-off from Jonathan, or so she thought. She squinted her eyes, pointed at him with three fingers, and walked away.

"What was that all about?" he asked me.

I answered in a matter-of-fact tone between sips of champagne. "She cursed you."

"She what?"

"Don't feel special," I said. "She'll curse half the people here before this night is over." I shrugged. "It's what she does."

Cassie laughed. "Placing a curse on your host *before* the free meal. Now, *there's* a sense of entitlement for ya."

"Okay," I said to my mother and Jonathan's father. "Let's have it. How do you two know each other? This is crazy."

Walter smiled. "I'm not sure where to start. Hmmm. Let's see. When we first met, I was a student at Columbia University."

"And I spent that summer in Greenwich Village," my mother added. "We were soooo in love."

Jonathan buried his face in his palms. "Oh, God."

I nudged him in the ribs with my elbow.

Walter took a sip of champagne.

"Dad, you don't drink champagne."

"I do occasionally—every thirty years or so." He and my mother giggled.

"You don't giggle either, Dad." Jonathan turned to me. "He's never giggled. He doesn't giggle. Now he's sitting there giggling? What is happening?"

"Getting this story out is like pulling teeth," Cassie said.

"It is. Keep going with the story, Mother."

My mother sipped from her glass. "There's not much to tell, really."

"Thank God," Jonathan and I said simultaneously.

"We were young and came from two different walks of life.

It was obvious Jonathan didn't want to hear another word, but he was stuck there. If he could dash away, I'm sure he would. As my mother spoke, he covered up his ears with both hands and sang la la la la la la la.

I dug my elbow into his side as a signal to stop. "A future Congressman doesn't do that."

Jonathan narrowed his eyes at me and removed his hands from his ears.

Walter continued. "Anyway, it didn't work out. My parents disapproved."

My mother said, "And my mother didn't dig his style—too uptight."

Walter laughed. "That's right. Her mother suggested I wear beads and sandals. Can you believe that, Son?"

"It happens," Jonathan said as he chugged a glass of champagne.

"So, you broke up?" Cassie asked.

Walter nodded. "We did. I graduated, met and married another girl, started a family," he pointed to Jonathan, "and moved to L.A."

"And there's your happy ending," I said, lifting my champagne glass.

Everyone clinked their glasses together except Jonathan. He drank directly out of the champagne bottle.

Jonathan whispered in my ear. "I don't know who this guy is. He is not my dad."

Walter gazed at my mother. "And what about you, Chipmunk? What brought you to California?"

"Acting classes," my mother said. "I was going to be a big star. But then I hooked up with someone and became pregnant with Piper. He didn't stick around long. So, in keeping with the tradition of the women in my family, I was a single mom and raised her all by myself. Piper was my life until she left home for law school, of all things." She reached out and squeezed Walter's hand. "Still, after all these years, Wally, you're the one that got away."

Jonathan held up an empty champagne bottle. "Waiter, one more, please!"

I patted Jonathan's leg under the table. "It'll be alright. Just relax."

"Wally, do you ever think of us?" my mother asked.

Jonathan jumped in. "Nope. He's been too busy to dwell on the past. Right, Dad?"

"At ease, soldier," Walter said to Jonathan. Now that's a question I don't normally like to answer, especially at a table full of people. But if I had to—if someone held a gun to my head—"

"Don't give Jonathan any ideas," I said.

Walter smiled at my mother. "Do I still think about those times? I'd have to admit, Chipmunk, that I do."

Jonathan's head hit the table.

My mother blushed at Walter's answer. She fanned her face with her hand. "Oh, my. Feelings I thought were long gone have suddenly resurfaced." She gazed into his eyes. "Wally, there's a beautiful moon in the sky, and soft music is playing. How about one more dance, for old time's sake?"

Jonathan picked his head up. "He can't. We're about to eat."

Walter rose from his chair, put his arm out, and escorted my mother to a corner of the courtyard, where they slow-danced.

All eyes were fixed on my mother and Walter as they moved in small circles.

For the first minute of the dancing exhibition, Jonathan was silent. But that didn't last for long. He leaned toward me. "He's not a dance guy. This is bizarre. What is happening here? I saw a Twilight Zone like this once."

"Okay, we need to keep calm," I said. "In a week or so, she'll be back home, he'll be back home, and the world will still be spinning."

"I feel a high-speed wobble coming on."

"That's the champagne."

"Seriously, Piper. There are three hundred and fifty million people in this country. And somehow, they know each other? Explain that. Especially given the fact that they're both opposites."

"People from different worlds meet all the time. Look at Beauty and the B—" I stopped short of completing the sentence.

Jonathan folded his arms and stared at me.

"How about Adam and Eve?" Cassie asked.

"They weren't different types," Jonathan said.

"Perfect example, Cass," I said. "Eve was a vegetarian, and my mother is too."

Jonathan rested his chin on his fist and frowned while his father danced. "And Eve's out there right now, trying to get him to take a bite. But this time, it's not an apple; it's a moon. We need to discourage this. No good can come from them being friends or—God help us—anything more than that."

I straightened my posture. "What do you mean, *she's* trying? *He's* out there too. Jonathan, you act like he's completely innocent."

"He *is* innocent. He thinks 50 Shades of Grey is a hair product for men. What does that tell you?"

I asked Cassie, "What do you think we should do?"

Cassie's eyes followed the two as they danced. "If I were you, I wouldn't be too quick to discourage them, but I don't think you need to encourage them, either."

Jonathan asked Howie for his opinion.

Howie nodded toward Cassie and said, "What *she* said." Howie punctuated his patronizing answer with a flirtatious smile at Cassie.

Jonathan frowned at Howie. "A lot of help you are."

"Cassie's right," I said. "They can be friendly without being friends. That would work for everybody."

Howie directed his attention toward the slow-dancing couple who were now lost in each other's eyes and said, "Then you better turn the music off."

"This is nuts," said Jonathan. "Look at him out there. This isn't the person that raised me. This isn't the guy who constantly asked me over the past five years, 'What would your mother be thinking right now?' Well, Dad, now I'm asking *you*. What would she be thinking right now?"

"It's okay, honey," I said while patting his arm. "You're letting your imagination get carried away."

"Oh, am I? I don't think so. He's not himself. He's out there dancing under the moon. The next thing I know, he'll be singing to the moon."

My mother and Walter returned to the table.

"That's Amore!" Walter belted out in song, using a horrendous Italian accent.

"F this! F this place! Dammit! What the hell?" a woman shouted.

My mother shrieked and clapped. "Tonya! You made it!"

CHAPTER 12

Jonathan turned and glared at me. "Is this Tanya, the one who's cured from Tourette's?"

"Yes. I mean *no*. I mean, yes, that's Tanya, and is she over her Tourette's? Maybe not."

As impulsive as Tanya was, it impressed me she was making progress by having the discipline and good sense not to pronounce the remaining portion of the F word—should there be children nearby.

Howie and my mother escorted Tanya to Florina and Cousin Cosmo's table.

My mother pointed to an empty chair at the table. "Here's your seat, Tanya. I'm thrilled you could make it. You're just in time for dinner."

Tanya sat at the table and pressed down on her bottom lip with her upper teeth, ready to blast any word beginning with the letter *F* at a moment's notice. She was locked and loaded with an arsenal of profane ammunition.

Cousin Cosmo filled his cape's pocket with silverware while Florina was busy staring into her crystal ball.

"Florina, Cosmo, say hi to Tanya," my mother urged.

Florina stopped studying her crystal ball long enough to say, "Oh, hi, Tanya."

"Forget you!" Tanya blurted.

My mother and Howie returned to the main table.

Howie stopped between me and Jonathan, bent down, and

whispered. "Jonathan, you got a bunch of screwballs here. Not a good image for someone running for congress."

"I'm sitting right here, Howie," I said.

Jonathan lifted his eyes at Howie. "Tell me about it."

"When I made my rounds earlier, I didn't see anyone from the media. If photos of your future in-laws get published, all bets are off. But so far, we're safe. There was a friendly guy in the bar with a telescopic lens on his camera, but don't worry. He said he was a nature photographer. Oh, and he liked the Dodgers too. My kind of guy."

That comment caught my attention. "What? Wait. How do you know he liked the Dodgers?"

"He had a blue Dodger cap on. Like I said—great guy."

Jonathan patted Howie on the shoulder. "Great job, Howie. We need to be careful that no one gets photos. I don't want to be explaining this group at my next press conference. Keep up the good work."

"Yeah, nothing gets by you, Howie," I said. I should have known better than to rely on Howie to secure the area. He wouldn't notice Malcom Hyde's limo if it were parked on the dance floor.

I leaned close to Cassie's ear and whispered, "We got big problems, Cass. That private eye is on the premises."

"The creep with the Dodger cap? You better tell Jonathan."

"No way. With all he's going through, he'll freak out. We need to handle this ourselves."

"How?"

I paused while I thought about how to answer her in a way that showed I had command of the situation. But nothing came to mind. I said, "I have no idea."

Two waiters arrived at the tables and prepared to serve dinner.

"I'm starving. I could eat a horse!" Walter said.

I chuckled. "Darn. The market was all out of horses. But we do have soup coming up."

Walter shrugged. "Soup? Fine. What's the main course?"

"There's a salad too," I said.

My mother nudged Walter. "I created the menu. Piper wanted to do it, but she finally gave in. I hope you like it."

"Soup and salad. Huh. Okay. That's a start," Walter said.

"No, Dad. That's it. That's what she planned," Jonathan said.

"Soup and salad? No entrée?"

My mother rubbed Walter's back. "Wally, it's more than just soup and salad. It's a very special recipe. And very healthy. I wanted our dinner theme to be all about *health*."

Walter frowned. "There's got to be more than that. Folks aren't going to be happy. Has Tanya seen the menu yet?"

A 300-pound bald man in his seventies and wearing a plaid suit approached the table. His arms were outstretched, just barely wider than his smile. "Harmony?"

My mother jumped up and giggled. "Uncle Arnold!"

Jonathan whispered in my ear, "Uh, wild guess here, but is he the term life insurance salesman?"

I clenched my jaw and nodded. "I thought Mother agreed not to invite him."

"She must've been feeling generous."

Uncle Arnold greeted each person at the table with a handshake and a pat on the back. When he reached Jonathan, he said, "Great to meet you finally. I've heard tons about you for years."

"Years?" Jonathan asked.

"Harmony is always yakking about what a fine young man you are. How responsible you are."

I forced a smile.

"I try to be," Jonathan said.

"Yesiree, a fine young man. I can tell you're the kind of guy who's not afraid to do the right thing. The kind of guy willing to forego expensive cars and shiny Rolex watches to budget your money with an eye on the future. I can see that quality in you."

Uncle Arnold's pitch mesmerized Howie. "Wow. He's awesome."

Uncle Arnold winked at Jonathan. "Yep, I gotta tell ya, you're just now starting out on the road of life, which means this is a critical time for decision making. You have quite an adventure ahead of you. You and the misses here—our sweet Paula—"

"Piper," I said.

"Whatever," said Uncle Arnold. "Anyway, you and Piper have a whole lot to think about."

"I'm thinking things right now," I admitted.

Uncle Arnold winked. "I'm sure you are. We never know what's in the cards for us. What's in our future. What fate has planned."

"I can always ask Florina," I said.

Uncle Arnold didn't appreciate my comment. I disrupted his train of thought.

He continued. "As I was saying, fate has a plan for you. But it's a secret plan you're not allowed to know. But that doesn't mean *you* can't plan."

Planning my guest list better is what popped into my mind.

Uncle Arnold continued. "Piper, if something unfortunate and unforeseeable happened to Jameson, God forbid, would you be okay?"

"Sure, because I worry mainly about… *Jonathan*."

Uncle Arnold popped himself in the forehead. "Right. *Jonathon*. Tomatoes—tomahtoes. But the question is still valid. Would you be okay, Piper?"

"I'd miss him. But I support myself now, so yes, I'd be okay."

"I wouldn't mind hearing more," said Howie.

Uncle Arnold's head swiveled toward Howie like a hawk who just spotted a mouse. "Son, let's take a walk. I think there are a few financial tips I can pass on to you—before *I* pass on."

Howie laughed at Uncle Arnold's line and agreed to take a short walk around the exterior of the courtyard to hear more words of wisdom.

"Howie, as the best man," Jonathan said, "don't you think you should stay here?"

"We won't be long," Uncle Arnold said.

"Can I walk with you two?" I asked. "I'm interested in financial planning."

"Sure!" Uncle Arnold said. "The more the merrier."

As I stood up, Jonathan tugged at my outfit. "Piper, are you serious? This is our wedding rehearsal! What the hell is happening to everyone?"

"I'll just be a minute." Then I leaned down to Cassie and whispered, "Keep an eye on Jonathan. And keep him off any high ledges. He's not holding up well. I'll be right back."

I walked behind Howie and Uncle Arnold.

Decorative pavers formed a curved walkway outside the courtyard walls. Uncle Arnold had his hand on Howie's shoulder as they walked. He was just getting into the details of setting up a term life insurance policy when Howie reacted to seeing Griggs standing on the walkway ahead. Griggs was aiming his camera's telephoto lens through the arched opening of the patio's exterior wall and directly at our guests.

"Hey, buddy!" Howie shouted to Griggs.

Griggs whirled around to see Howie approaching. His expression revealed he knew he'd been caught. He lowered his camera and was about to run away when Howie spoke again.

"Uncle Arnold and Piper, let me introduce you to my friend here in the Dodger cap. I met him earlier in the bar."

Griggs froze.

Howie shook Griggs' hand. "How's it going, buddy?"

Griggs was tongue-tied but managed to say, "Alright."

"Uncle Arnold here was filling us in on how to cover any burial costs that might arise."

Uncle Arnold stepped forward and shook Grigg's hand. "Are your burial cost covered?"

Griggs said to Howie, "Is this your enforcer?"

Howie studied Uncle Arnold and said, "Hmmm. Technically, it would be my policy, and as long as I continue to pay him, it's enforced. Is that what you mean?"

Grigg's eyes widened. "Dude, I don't want no trouble. I'm just doin' a job. It's not personal."

Howie pointed at the camera with the long lens. "That's quite

CHAPTER 12

a camera he's got there," he said to Uncle Arnold. "His hobby is nature photography."

"Huh?" Griggs responded. "Oh, right. The bar conversation."

"Nature photography?" Uncle Arnold asked Griggs. "I'm sure there's plenty of danger in photographing animals in the wild. You need to make sure your loved ones are financially secure should a big ape pounce on you."

"Okay. I get it. I can read between the lines. Big ape pouncing on me? Is that a threat?"

Uncle Arnold scratched his head while he turned to Howie and me. "What's he talking about?"

Griggs walked backwards, away from us. "Don't play dumb with me, you big ape. I've dealt with enforcers like you plenty." He pointed his camera at us and snapped several photos.

Uncle Arnold, a true salesman, didn't give up. "Look. I'm just trying to help you. We're all going to end up six feet underground sooner or later. I hope your time will be later, I really do. But you never know. The decisions you make tonight will make a difference to your loved ones."

Griggs continued to back up. He patted his camera. "I got what I need right here. Yeah. I'll get a good price for the shots I've captured."

Sherman hurried out of the men's room and collided into Griggs, knocking his camera to the floor where it shattered into a hundred pieces.

Griggs shrieked and sprinted away.

Sherman shouted, "Sorry!"

I clenched my fist and said, "Yes!"

Howie said to Sherman, "That camera was that nature photographer's livelihood. You need to watch where you're going."

Uncle Arnold shook his head as Griggs disappeared into the night. He turned to Howie and asked, "You don't happen to have his phone number, do you?"

Howie agreed to schedule an appointment with Uncle Arnold, and we all headed back to the main table. Not much had changed. Walter continued to complain about the dinner. "No comfort food? No steak? No meat and potatoes? Not even a pot roast?"

"I'm a vegan," my mother answered.

Walter smirked. "Of course you are."

"What does *that* mean?"

"Look. I was just hoping for some comfort food. Is that a crime?"

"Comfort food? I don't find eating meat very comforting. I'm sure the animals don't either."

I sat next to Jonathan.

"Thank God you're back," Jonathan said. "This is getting crazy."

I patted him on the arm and turned to my mother. "Let's change the subject."

Jonathan nudged me. "No, let's not." He nodded toward our parents, who were glaring at each other. "This is good. I like this subject."

Walter tossed his napkin on the table. "There was a day when people served meatloaf or a pot roast. I guess those days are gone."

My mother lifted her chin and closed her eyes. "Thankfully. We're trying to save the planet."

"Here we go," I moaned.

Walter became angrier. "How in the hell does a pot roast destroy the planet?"

Tanya observed Walter and my mother from her table and said, "Yeah, and they're worried about my Tourette's."

My mother said, "I'm not going down this road. It's a beautiful evening. Let's not ruin it."

"Please," Jonathan encouraged, "let's go down this road."

Walter said, "I'm sitting here at a rehearsal dinner, and there's only soup? It all started going downhill when I learned the wedding was at the beach and not in a church."

"God is at the beach too, you know," my mother said.

"He won't be tomorrow. He'll be waiting at the church."

"Oh, so God's a man?"

"A man who plenished the earth with plenty of pot roast walking around."

My mother narrowed her eyes. "Pot roast. Ha! Saving the planet is a complicated subject. Too complicated for you!"

"Bread, Mother?" I asked.

Walter smirked. "Because I'm, apparently, a knuckle-dragging simpleton, why don't you uncomplicate it for me?"

My mother leaned back in her chair, folded her arms, and closed her eyes. "It's all coming back now. Oh, yeah."

"Look," said Walter, "I'm not hard to please. My wife—rest her soul—wasn't a great cook, but she tried. Did I complain once? No. On Thanksgiving, did I say a word when some of the cranberry sauce still retained the ridges of the can? No."

I whispered to Jonathan, "Take their steak knives."

"Some people never change," Walter said, staring straight at my mother.

"Some people refuse to change," she said. "Wally, you are impossible!"

"*I'm* impossible? You're intolerant of any opinion that doesn't match yours!"

My mother stood. "Ask anyone. I'm kind and loving and easy to get along with."

Walter scoffed. "Fine. Let's ask your twelve ex-boyfriends."

The hostile direction of their conversation horrified me.

Even under all that makeup were the flushed cheeks of my mother's face. "If anyone cares, I'll be in my room." She stormed off.

Walter stood and marched away in the opposite direction.

Jonathan leaned back in his chair and grinned.

CHAPTER 13

I blinked my sleepy eyes open as they adjusted to the gray morning light flooding through the bridal suite window. Voices from the TV I left on for white noise awakened me. The day was finally here! It was too good to be true. I've waited my whole life for this. It was the day I'd marry the love of my life. Or, more accurately, the love of my last two months.

I tried my best to forget the events of the night before. Still, the rehearsal dinner from hell was fresh in my mind. My mother had locked herself in her seventh-floor room and refused to talk to anyone. Walter sat outside alone near the hotel pool and puffed on a cigar until two in the morning. The couple that didn't speak for thirty years was still not speaking. Jonathan probably slept like a baby. Walter and my mother's argument doused any chance of them rekindling their old flame, which surely enabled Jonathan to get a good night's rest.

Last night, I needed someone to talk to, but Cassie didn't answer her mobile phone for several hours. I forced myself to close my eyes and finally fell asleep.

As far as I was concerned, the nightmare evening was behind us, and it was a brand-new day. It would be the most special day ever.

Someone knocked on the door. I crossed the room, stood in silence at the door, and shouted, "Jonathan, if that's you, you're not supposed to see me before the ceremony! It's bad luck!"

"It's me. Cassie."

Still in my nightgown, I unlocked the door.

Cassie walked in and scoffed. "Bad luck? If you're trying to avoid bad luck, that ship has sailed, girl."

Cassie carried two cups full of coffee. She handed one to me, and we sat on the bed.

"I tried to call you last night. You didn't answer," I said.

"I called you back, but you were probably asleep."

"What was going on?"

Cassie giggled. "I went to the police station with Howie."

"And why would you do that?"

"Late last night, some of the guests your mother invited ended up in jail."

"What? Who was arrested?"

"Cousin Cosmo got arrested for stealing the hotel's silverware, and Tonya faced charges for interfering with police work after she launched into a profanity-laced tirade at the arresting officer. Uncle Arnold followed the squad car to the police station to pitch a term life plan to the jailer—and actually closed the sale. And my mother said Florina claimed she saw it all two days earlier in her crystal ball. Jonathan dispatched Howie to the police station to post everyone's bail.

I covered my mouth with my hand. "No way. Oh my God!"

"Believe me, Piper, I couldn't make this stuff up."

I was sick to my stomach. Putting Jonathan through that might have been the straw that broke the camel's back. I leaned back against the headboard and groaned. "Jonathan's going to kill me. Or kill my mother. Either way, somebody's going down."

Cassie said, "When Howie asked if I wanted to go with him to the jail, I said yes. It was exciting. Like being on that TV show, *Cops*. Howie can be pretty cool."

I blinked hard a few times. In the same sentence, Cassie used the words *Howie* and *cool*. I needed a moment to process that. I tried to study Cassie's face, but Cassie avoided eye contact. "Is something going on between you and Howie?"

"No. He's just interesting, that's all."

I tilted my head to understand her words. "Is there another Howie here at the hotel?"

Cassie shook her head.

"You're talking about *our* Howie—best man Howie?"

"Yeah. Why?"

"You used the word *interesting*."

"Yeah. I think he's interesting."

"*Interesting* as in… this solid beige paper coffee cup sure is interesting."

"That's right. How would *you* describe him?"

"I don't know if I'd use that word. When I hear the word *interesting*, I expect it to be used in the context of something like—the sight of that solid beige paper coffee cup held by that Martian while he stands in the doorway of his flying saucer, sure is interesting."

Cassie pointed at the TV. "Look!"

On the TV screen, a news reporter held a microphone while he stood on the beach. The wind was whipping his hair and tie. "Looks like the storm that was supposed to stay to the north of us has a mind of its own and has taken a more southerly path. The latest radar shows it moving ashore in the next hour. With any luck, this weather system will quickly move through the area and be gone in the next twenty-four hours. Back to you in the studio."

"Storm? What?" I shouted at the TV.

"This can't be happening," Cassie said.

I jumped up and ran to the window. I peered down at the beach. "Oh, God!" I threw on a robe and pink fuzzy slippers and ran out of the room. "C'mon!"

Cassie chased me down the hallway to where a man was waiting for the elevator door to open. I pushed the button repeatedly for a minute straight because that always helps.

"Where are we going?" Cassie asked.

I didn't answer. The elevator door finally opened, and we rode it down to the lobby. I ran through the lobby and out the hotel's entrance. The sky was full of fast-moving black clouds, and the hotel's flags flapped in the wind.

I dashed across the grounds and onto the sandy beach,

occasionally glancing back at Cassie. She was bent over with her hands on her knees, trying to catch her breath.

A small crew had already dismantled half the wedding site, and I ran toward them like a crazed woman. They placed folding chairs in several stacks. The wind had blown away most of the flowers on the no-longer-lush floral wedding arch.

I screamed at the workers. "What are you doing?"

One of them tried to answer over the noise of the crashing waves and howling wind. "The weather! Sorry, but your wedding—it ain't gonna happen! Not here! Not today!"

"It's not going to rain!" I insisted.

While holding his hat on his head, a worker said, "I got the weather update! One hundred percent chance! No one expected this. Sorry!"

Emotion rose in my throat, and my sight blurred with tears. Cassie finally caught up and put her arm around me.

"This is not fair!" I shouted. "All I've ever wanted was to get married, but everything's working against me."

Debris swirled in the air. Something landed at my feet, and the wind kept it pinned against my ankles. I reached down and grabbed it—a square hat with a galaxy logo on the front.

"That's mine!" Brother Larry shouted as he walked toward us.

I plopped down on the sand, held my head down, and cried a steady stream of tears. When Brother Larry reached me, I raised his hat high above my head without looking at him.

He took his hat and shouted over the wind and waves, "The wedding can't happen here at the beach! And the hotel is already booked with two weddings!"

I couldn't speak. Helpless, I held my arms out and shook my head before trudging back to the hotel, with Cassie propping me up.

Once inside my room, I collapsed face first on the bed.

"I'll call your mother and tell her the wedding is postponed," Cassie said.

The word *postponed* hit me like a stale wedding cake. Just when things couldn't get worse, they did. Without a doubt, this was the worst thing that could happen. But I didn't want to exaggerate, so I decided that a nuclear attack would probably be the worst thing that could happen. But having my wedding postponed was a close second.

"She's not answering," Cassie said.

I buried my face in a pillow and screamed several muffled phrases containing not one decipherable word.

Cassie rolled me over until I was face up. "What are you saying?"

I groaned for another minute. Then I asked, "What time is it?"

Cassie checked her watch. "Nine-thirty."

"Why isn't she answering her damn phone? Would you call Jonathan for me and tell him to come here?"

"Of course. And I'll find your mother. Don't worry. Everything's going to work out. It's just a weather delay, that's all." She brushed the tangled hair from my face. "But honestly, my heart breaks for you. You've worked very hard on your wedding day plans. To have it all yanked away from you at the last minute is just awful."

"It's cruel and unusual punishment. And that's supposed to be unconstitutional."

"You're not inside a courtroom. Mother nature's laws trump our man-made laws."

I ran to the balcony and leaned on the railing. "I object!" I shouted at the sky. "I object to this storm!"

Cassie put her arm around me and brought me back to my bed. Her voice cracked with emotion. "If I could, I'd snap my fingers and create a perfectly sunny day custom-made for a wedding. Piper, you know I'd give up a limb if it would make everything right." She paused to think for a moment and revised her pledge. "Well, giving up a limb is a lot to ask. But I *would* still do the finger snap thing if it would bring a sunny day. I'd do that."

Cassie answered a knock on the door while I sobbed.

It was Jonathan.

"Hi, Jonathan," Cassie said as she hugged him. "I'm sorry

about the weather."

"Thanks, Cass. I appreciate you. You're a great friend to both of us."

"I'll leave you two alone." She turned to me and said, "I'll be in my room. Call if you need me, hun."

As she left, Cassie shut the door behind her.

Jonathan sat on the edge of the bed. "Piper, baby, I'm here."

I sat up and fell into his arms. Jonathan held me tight. My face was puffy and swollen from crying, and he placed tender little kisses on my forehead and my cheeks.

"It'll be alright. Don't worry. What's that saying? When you're busy making other plans, life happens. That's all this is. Just a temporary setback."

"I'm afraid if we don't get married right away, we never will."

He pulled a tissue from a box on the nightstand and handed it to me.

I wiped my eyes. "Everything's gone wrong. All my planning either turned into a disaster or was washed away by the rain."

Jonathan half-smiled and teased, "It's that curse Florina put on me. It's all her fault."

My sobbing eased up for a moment, and I laughed a little. "I'm sorry for everything that's gone wrong. I am."

"It's alright. We still have each other. We'll regroup and try again tomorrow. It's only one day."

"I can't risk waiting another day."

Jonathan angled his head to see my face. "What do you mean by that?"

I dabbed my eyes and nose with the tissue. "The way things are going, I'm afraid that if any more time goes by, you'll find a reason not to marry me."

"Don't be silly. That would never happen."

"Sweetie," I said, "I can't imagine going through life without you as my partner. I don't know what I'd do if we didn't marry."

He tightened his arms to bring me closer to him. "You should know this; *I'm* the one who can't exist without you. If I couldn't spend every day for the rest of my life at your side, I'd be lost and wouldn't know which way to turn. I love you so much. I love you much more than you'll ever know. A one-day delay makes no difference to me."

My fingers slowly traced his stubbled jawline. "I love you, Jonathan. And I'll love you forever."

His face turned more serious. "Just promise me one thing."

"Anything."

He gazed deeply into my teary eyes. "Promise me you won't wear those pink fuzzy slippers in public ever again."

He laughed, and I picked up a pillow and playfully hit him with it.

Jonathan's mobile phone rang, and he read the screen. "It's Howie." Jonathan spoke into the phone. "What's up?"

Jonathan listened for a minute and grimaced. He closed his eyes, ended the call, and said, "Your mother and my father were seen jumping into a cab this morning."

CHAPTER 14

Jonathan jammed his phone back into his pocket. "I thought we were past this problem last night."

"They took a cab?" I asked. "Where would they be going? My mother knows I'm getting married today." I paused and revised that statement. "Well, *they* think I'm getting married today. My mother should be right here, carrying out her role as the bride's mother."

"You're right. Who's going to cause trouble, provide awkward moments, and dish out backhanded compliments?"

"Not funny."

"You're right. It's not. And I agree one hundred percent. They should be here. I'm very uncomfortable with those two having a cozy friendship. They need to get back to feeling contempt for each other, like normal in-laws." Jonathan stopped and stared out the hotel room window. "Nothing good can come from this. The last time we saw them, they were at each other's throats. That was a good thing. And now they're in some cab going God knows where."

His worrying about our parents was a little over the top, so I said, "We should have had Girl Scout Chrissy watch them."

"Yes. Of the three, she would've been the one with the most common sense—and she's eleven."

"My mother wasn't answering her phone this morning, which is weird, especially on this day. Just call your dad and see what's going on. Maybe there's a good explanation and nothing to worry about."

Jonathan dialed Walter. No answer.

Jonathan's face turned dead serious. "I don't want to worry you, but maybe he kidnapped her. This kind of stuff is on the news all the time."

"You know you're losing your mind, right? This is your dad you're talking about."

"I'm not sure about that anymore. I thought I knew my dad. The guy in the cab with your mother is somebody else."

"Jonathan, would you please stop? You're freaking me out. I'm sure it's innocent. After last night, they probably went to breakfast to make amends."

"Naw, that's what normal people would do."

"Well, let's look at it this way," I said. "If they patch things up and accept each other's differences, future Thanksgivings won't be a nightmare."

Jonathan was half serious when he insisted that the enigma who resembled his father and jumped in the cab was no one he knew. This was not the behavior his dad ever exhibited in Jonathan's memory, even once. "Harmony's type was not anything my dad would have tolerated in the past. She's a loose cannon, and he runs a tight ship." Jonathan paced back and forth, talking to himself. "Did he finally snap? No, that's not possible. He doesn't have a violent bone in his body. If you asked his neighbors, they'd all say he was the quiet type—grouchy and maybe in a perpetual bad mood—but quiet and reserved, nonetheless. Oh, God—that's the very thing they say about someone who snapped and made the evening news. *We were so surprised; he was the quiet type who kept to himself.*"

"Stay calm, sweetie. You're letting your imagination get carried away."

He spun toward me. His eyes were wide with fright. "A terrible image just flashed across my mind!"

"An image?"

"Oh, God. I was standing in the desert near a newly discovered shallow grave. It was cordoned off by police caution tape. We were both there, and I was trying to explain to you that the upside to the horrific find was that future Thanksgivings would be peaceful. And you weren't all that understanding!"

Jonathan's craziness was starting to affect me. How worried should I be? I mean, I've only met Walter a few times. I really didn't know him. But I was calmed by the thought that my mother was tough and could take care of herself. Even if a dangerous alien from outer space took over Walter's body, I was confident in my mother's ability to handle it. And considering her history of totally demoralizing past partners, any concern should be for the alien.

Yes, Jonathan's concern was misplaced. He should be worried about what my mother might do, not his father. My mind rifled through several scenarios. Did she concoct some scheme decades ago after Walter broke up with her? Was she planning a morning walk with him on the pier, only to return alone? Never underestimate a jilted woman. I imagined her peering over the pier's railing and savoring every moment of the shark attack that made quick work of Walter. Of course, every jilted woman has such thoughts, but few of us rarely carry them out. But could my mother be one of the *few*?

I had to get hold of myself. My thoughts were getting crazy. Thank God they were all in my head and not out loud like Jonathan's were.

I said to Jonathan, "You need to calm down. Listen to how crazy you sound."

"I'm telling you, your mother put a spell on my dad."

A spell? Was that even possible? Maybe.

Jonathan walked to the sliding glass door of the veranda and scanned the beach. I joined him. The wind howled and what remained of the wedding arch was now leaning to one side. I tried to keep my tears from flowing, but I couldn't. I was frustrated, sad, and now filled with worry over the whereabouts of my mother and Walter. Jonathan wrapped his arms around me and held me.

His phone rang and interrupted the tender moment. He pulled it out of his pocket and put it on speaker mode.

It was Howie again. "Hey, it's me. Cassie gave me the guest list. Sherman and I are downstairs in the coffee shop, calling everyone to let them know you postponed the wedding for one day."

"Thank you, buddy."

Howie continued. "Just so you know, I've seen a few more things that have caused some concern."

"What now?"

"Piper's relative, the one in the cape—"

"Cousin Cosmo?"

"That's the guy. He came back here after I bailed him out. He's here in the hotel coffee shop with that foul-mouthed woman who could make a sailor blush—"

"Tonya?"

"Yep. Looks like she wasn't happy with her omelet and called the waitress every name in the book. Tanya mentioned your name several times."

Jonathan turned to me. "Great. It looks like your nutty relatives are not leaving."

I shrugged my shoulders. "Not much we can do."

"The good news is," Howie said, "they're the only ones I see—hold on a minute. That woman with the crystal ball and the term life insurance salesman are here, too."

"Florina and Uncle Arnold," I said.

Howie continued. "Yeah, that's them. Uncle Arnold has a hotel employee cornered, showing her a pamphlet. I gotta admit, he's one determined salesman. Anyway, I haven't seen any reporters or snoops from Hyde's office here, so we don't have to worry about any negative headlines."

Griggs' voice flowed from the phone's speaker as he spoke to Howie. "Your friend here broke my camera."

Jonathan's eyes shifted to me, and his brows raised. I shrugged my shoulders, pretending I had no idea what was happening or who that was.

"It was an accident," Sherman said.

Griggs said, "Accident, my ass. You're lucky, kid. You're lucky I have a new camera being delivered here today, or I'd sue you for loss of income."

Howie asked, "You were on assignment last night? I thought you photographed wild animals."

"Have you looked around this coffee shop?" Griggs asked.

Then Uncle Arnold's voice joined in. "Hey, there you are!"

"Stay away from me!" Griggs shouted.

Uncle Arnold said, "We never finished our talk last night! Insurance will get your loved ones through an unfortunate event."

Footsteps pounded.

Howie said, "Uncle Arnold never gives up. He just chased that nature photographer out of the coffee shop."

Jonathan said to me, "Your uncle needs to back off a bit."

I nodded.

Jonathan spoke into the phone. "Okay, Howie. Keep up the good work."

As he hung up, I shook my head and put a puzzled expression on my face.

The rest of the day passed without incident, mainly because we locked ourselves in my hotel room and napped the day away in a spooning position, only waking to receive deliveries from room service.

Occasionally, I'd dial my mother.

Finally, she answered. "Hi sweetie, I can't talk now. I'll call you right back."

But she didn't call back. Jonathan received pretty much the same response when he dialed the space alien—or whoever was occupying his dad's body.

Jonathan and I found it unsettling that our parents were acting so weird. We were somewhat relieved that my mother wasn't in a shallow grave and Walter wasn't shark bait.

Jonathan grabbed a bottle of water from the mini-fridge. As he walked past the balcony, he stopped to look out at the rain.

The afternoon was growing dark. He was about to return to my side when he stopped. Someone was on the beach. Someone in a yellow raincoat stood near the emaciated wind-blown floral wedding arch. Jonathan kept an eye on the suspicious person, making sure the nutcase wasn't vandalizing what remained of tomorrow's wedding site. A moment later, another person in a red raincoat crossed the sand and spoke to yellow raincoat. Red raincoat turned and pointed to an approaching figure in a blue raincoat. The three had a conversation near the wind-blown wedding arch. Yellow raincoat appeared to be giving instructions to the others.

"Piper, are you having anyone repair the wedding site?"

I walked out onto the veranda and peered down at the beach. The covered balcony was only partially protecting me from the slanting rain. "Yes, but they weren't supposed to start until morning," I shouted back to Jonathan.

"Right. What's the point of doing anything in the middle of this storm?"

I stepped back into the room and shut the sliding glass door. "Oh well. They'll just have to come back in the morning and fix any additional damage."

I continued to monitor the beach. Sheets of rain pelted the hotel as the crew conversed on the sand. It wasn't long until the crew in raincoats, after much discussion, surrendered to the rain. They left the arch and headed back across the sand toward the hotel.

I sat on the sofa and pointed the remote-control device at the TV. "I better check the weather channel. This rain is relentless." After wading through an endless stream of commercials selling weather-related products like car floor mats, rain gutter leaf guards, and weatherproof caulk, the anchor finally appeared on the screen and pointed to a radar map of New England. "Yeah, that's helpful—not."

"Try the local news," Jonathan suggested.

I pointed the remote at the TV again and changed channels.

The anchor on the local news said, "There's a brief lull in The

Naked Strangler Case—" I clicked the remote again and jumped to another local channel. "I have enough to think about. That subject can wait."

The news anchor on Channel 4 was in the middle of a story. "Poll numbers are tightening in the local race for congress, and that has Congressman Malcolm Hyde worried." The station cut to a live shot of a reporter on a Santa Barbara city street, pointing a microphone toward Hyde as he opened the door of a luxury sedan.

"Worried?" laughed Hyde. "Not for a minute. Have you heard my opponent's ridiculous ideas? Jonathan Knight is obsessed with things like making the streets safer. Ha! Like that's ever going to happen! What a jackass. Every once in a while, somebody like Knight comes along, all straight-laced and pretending to be as pure as the freshly driven snow. Inevitably, something always surfaces, proving otherwise. I suspect it'll be no different with this fool, Jonathan Knight. We'll discover something. You'll see. There's a skeleton in every closet."

The reporter turned back toward the camera. "Back to you in the studio."

"We reached out to Jonathan Knight," the studio anchor said, "but he was unavailable for comment."

"Hey! No one reached out to me," Jonathan said.

The news anchor turned to his co-anchor. "Molly, this race is going to get interesting."

"Yes, it is, Doug. Let's just hope it doesn't get too ugly. In other news—"

I turned the TV off.

Jonathan had a look of concern on his face.

I said, "Don't let that make you paranoid, honey. Everything's fine. You're fine. And I've checked your closet. There's no skeleton in there. You have nothing scandalous to worry about."

Knock-knock-knock!

"I'll get it. Howie probably watched the same channel, too," Jonathan said as he opened the door.

Standing in the doorway, in a yellow raincoat, was Brother

Larry. He was soaked and even more nervous than usual.

"That was you down there on the beach?" Jonathan asked.

I joined Jonathan at the door. "Brother Larry, it's not your job to clean up the wedding site."

Brother Larry cleared his throat and swallowed. "Piper, Jonathan, I'd like to present, for the first time, Mr. Walter Knight…"

Walter stepped into the doorway. He was grinning and wearing a blue raincoat.

"Dad? What's going on?"

Brother Larry continued. "…and Mrs. Harmony Knight."

My mother, wearing a soaked red raincoat, stepped into full view next to Walter. She jutted her hand toward me, revealing a massive diamond ring. "We got married!" she joyfully shouted.

CHAPTER 15

Jonathan and I were speechless. Neither moved an inch.

It took a few seconds before I finally formed the words with my mouth. "You did what?"

Jonathan turned to me and smirked. "They're joking." He paused a moment. Then asked me, "Why aren't you laughing?"

"Because it's not funny," I replied.

"We're serious. We got married on the beach five minutes ago," my mother giggled.

Brother Larry verified the crazy story with a nod.

"Mother, tell me you didn't. Tell me you didn't get married!"

She chuckled. "It's true."

Jonathan threw his hands up. "Dad! What the hell?"

Walter pulled her closer. "Love is a strange and mysterious thing."

Jonathan turned to Brother Larry. "You performed the ceremony?"

Brother Larry held up a wad of bills. "Cash. Upfront."

"Was my dad coherent? Were his pupils dilated? Did you test his mental acuity with a simple question?"

"He *did* answer a simple question," said Brother Larry. "He answered, 'I do, Chipmunk.' That was good enough for me."

I staggered back into the hotel room and collapsed on the sofa. "This can't be happening! Mother, how could you do this? It's just too weird. I refuse to believe this."

Jonathan pulled Walter into the room. Before he closed the door, he said to Brother Larry, "Just—just go back to your room and wait there. And don't mention this to anyone." As Brother Larry walked away, Jonathan stuck his head into the hallway, checked in both directions, and shut the door.

I said, "Let me see that ring. I'm sure it's not real. We're being punked."

My mother walked over to the sofa and dangled her hand in front of me.

"I bet that ring is from a novelty shop at the pier," Jonathan said. "They bought it just for the practical joke. Probably cost five bucks."

I examined the diamond. Then flashed a troubled look toward Jonathan. "It looks like it might be real."

Walter sat in a soft chair. "The money I spent on it was real; I'll tell you that."

Jonathan closed his eyes. "I'm dreaming. That's what's going on. I'm having a bad dream. I'll wake up in a minute; I just know it."

"*I'm* the one living the dream," my mother said.

"You absolutely cannot be married!" Jonathan shouted. "My public image as a normal person with a normal family is ruined! Couldn't you have just gone steady first?"

"We already did that—years ago," Walter said.

"Dad, you both are opposite types! What were you thinking?" Jonathan turned toward my mother. "Harmony, he's all wrong for you! Somewhere out there is a guy with a man bun, a fishnet tank top, and nipple rings!"

"Maybe so," she said, "but I can't find him. So, as they say, if you can't be with the one you love, love the one you're with. Stephen Stills—1970."

I stretched both hands out in front of me in a self-calming gesture. "I'm not going to get too upset because I know this is a big prank on us. Right, Mother?"

My mother said, "Walter called me first thing this morning and apologized. He invited me to breakfast, and we just got to talking about how we were so in love at one time. That's when the big question popped up."

"You said *yes*?" I asked.

"*He* said yes," my mother explained. "*I* popped the question."

Jonathan said to me, "She popped the question. You and your mother are more alike than you think."

My mother said, "The only difference is, I didn't hire an airplane pulling a proposal banner. That's a little too weird for me."

I began to cry. "Mother, how could you do this? I'm getting married tomorrow. Did you forget?"

"I didn't forget at all. That's one of the things we talked about. Right, Wallypog?"

"He's not *Wallypog!* Or *Wally!* His name is Walter," Jonathan said.

"We sure did, Chipmunk."

My mother shot a flirty smile at Walter for agreeing so readily. "Once we made up our mind to get hitched, we realized the wedding arch was still on the beach, and Brother Larry was hanging around with nothing to do, so the decision to pull the trigger was a no-brainer."

"If only someone *would've* pulled a trigger," Jonathan added.

"But you need a wedding license first," I said.

Walter nodded. "That's what took us so long today. But fortunately, you can obtain a wedding license and get married on the same day in this county."

"There *should* be a waiting period," Jonathan said while pacing. "A cautionary cooling-off period—like there is when buying an exploding suicide jacket." Jonathan plopped onto the sofa next to me. "I don't get it, Dad. You've always been my rock. Mr. Stability. Mr. Common Sense. Now, I don't know what to expect next from you. What's your next move? A roadie for Shakira?"

"Who?" Walter asked.

My mother nudged Walter. "Now's probably not the time to mention the tattoo, Wally."

"You didn't!" I blurted.

"It's the craziest thing," Walter said. "Still hurts." He leaned to one side, lifting a butt cheek off the chair.

"Mother, did you steal my idea? Say you didn't!"

My mother grinned.

"You both got your initials tattooed on your asses! You did, didn't you?"

"*He* got tattooed today, not me," my mother said, smiling at Walter. "He's been on *my* ass for thirty years."

Walter laughed. "When she showed me my initials on her... uh... behind, that's what convinced me she loved me. I had no choice but to do the same."

"Are we in high school now?" Jonathan asked. He turned to me. "I told you. That's not my dad. It's an alien in my dad's body!"

My mother perked up. "Oooh, I could get into that."

"Gee, thanks, Mother. You stole my tattoo idea. Then you used my beach wedding location just one day before I'm supposed to get married. What's next? And by the way, when did you two have time for a tattoo session?"

"Today. We did a lot today," Walter answered.

Jonathan faced me while he pointed at Walter. "In one day, he attended his own wedding, apparently shopped at a jewelry store, and entered a tattoo parlor. This is the same guy who used to be overwhelmed remembering which day of the week was trash day."

"Okay," I said. "This is crazy, but it's not the end of the world. We all need to stay calm." I patted Jonathan on his arm.

Jonathan threw his hands up in the air. "Well, that pretty much does it. We can't get married."

"Whoa-whoa-whoa-whoa-whoa!" I shouted. "Why not?"

"Think," Jonathan answered. "We're now step-siblings."

"Technically speaking, maybe," my mother added.

I jumped to my feet. "Mother! What have you done?"

"Everybody, calm the hell down," Walter demanded. "Okay, yes, you could consider yourselves step-siblings, but there's no law that prohibits you from marrying. You're both independent adults with completely different sets of parents. I'm sure it happens all the time. I'm sure it's very common."

"So is diarrhea, but most people try to avoid it," Jonathan said.

My mother grabbed a nail file off the coffee table and filed her nails. "Let's not get carried away here. Someday, this will all be a funny story you'll tell."

"She's right," I said as I turned to Jonathan. "The only thing that should matter to us right now is our wedding tomorrow."

Jonathan became despondent as he sat on the sofa. He leaned forward, elbows on his knees, and hung his head. "I don't know what to think right now. I feel like running away."

I rolled my eyes. "Oh, brother."

"Could you please use another expression?" Jonathan asked.

I sat down next to him. "Your dad is right. Their marriage is *their* thing and has nothing to do with us and our relationship. Once we're married, we'll be just like any other couple. No different than... uh... Ben Affleck and Jennifer Garner."

"Divorced," my mother said.

"Okay, you know I don't keep up with celebrity news. Guilty as charged. Anyway, we'll be just like Brad Pitt and Jennifer Aniston."

"Sorry. Divorced," she said.

"Brad Pitt and Angelina Jolie?"

"The big D," chuckled my mother.

"Brad Pitt and Kim Kardashian."

"Well, not divorced."

"Ah ha!" I shouted. "See? Jonathan and I will be a normal married couple, just like them."

My mother held up her index finger. "The only reason they're not divorced is because they're not a couple. But would definitely be divorced if they were."

"Mother! You're not helping make my case. And neither is Brad Pitt."

Jonathan exhaled. "We need to put everything on hold."

"No-no-no-no-no-no-no," I said as I wrapped my arms around him. "We'll get through this. Everything's going to be fine. You'll see."

"Piper, I just want a normal life. Is that too much to ask?"

"I want that too."

Jonathan stood up and threw his arms out. "But now you're technically my step-sister."

"Not my doing."

"Still, this is too weird for me. Look, do I have to remind everyone I'm running as the grounded, common-sense candidate? Of all the things I'd like to accomplish, promoting incest is not high on my list!"

"This is California; no one will be shocked," said my mother while picking at a hangnail.

"It won't be incest. We're not blood relatives," I insisted.

I flashed Jonathan a sympathetic look and said, "I think what we need right now is to take a walk and get some fresh air." I faced away from my mother and Walter. "You know, be amongst *normal* people."

Jonathan stood up. "Maybe you're right. Fresh air would do me some good."

As we walked toward the door, Jonathan turned back toward his dad and my mother. "Don't do anything. Don't get any more crazy ideas. And stay away from the window. I don't need to see you two on the news tonight."

CHAPTER 16

Cassie, Howie, and the wedding party made last-minute plans to spend the evening at a bar in the center of Santa Barbara on State Street. Jonathan cautioned Howie to keep everyone under control. Jonathan feared that bridesmaids, groomsmen, music, a full moon, and colorful cocktails were a dangerous mix. Still, for some reason, they all voted on the State Street outing instead of Jonathan's suggestion, which was a lovely evening at his expense: a paperback book of their choice from the hotel gift shop and a generous supply of lightly salted rice cakes to enjoy in the solitary confinement of their separate hotel rooms.

I convinced Jonathan to spend the evening with our newly wedded parents at a quiet restaurant somewhere in town. It was my desperate attempt to normalize a situation that was far from normal. It took quite a bit of convincing, but Jonathan finally agreed. I think the only reason he did is to keep an eye on them.

Jonathan and I waited for my mother and Walter to join us in the hotel lobby. I wore a two-button blazer over a white blouse, black pants, and heels. Jonathan dressed in slacks, a white dress shirt, and black patent leather dress shoes.

Jonathan lowered his voice and whispered in my ear. "Remember the deal. Your mother and my dad must promise not to engage in PDA because that would provide TMI for that POS Malcolm Hyde, which would render my political aspirations DOA."

I pulled back with a curious expression. "Why are you talking like that?"

"In case anyone's listening."

With a straight face, I said, "Uh... FYI: BTW, you're sounding crazy, so knock that off ASAP.

"Here we are!" my mother shouted as she ran toward us. At least she *appeared* to be running. Her arms were pumping back and forth, her steps were quick and lively, and her hat was slipping off her head from the hectic motion, but in reality, she was moving at the speed of someone on a casual evening stroll. Her outfit was a walking advertisement for the bohemian look: a boldly colored paisley maxi dress with a wide waistband, spaghetti strap buttoned camisole top, straw tote bag to match the straw fedora, sheer turquoise flowing kimono, over-sized jewelry, and chunky-heeled plum-colored sandals. "Step lively, Wally! We're running behind!"

Ten feet behind her was an out-of-breath Walter.

"Oh, God," Jonathan mumbled at the sight of his dad.

Walter wore a dark gray suit, a blue tie, and a turquoise bracelet that he was unsuccessfully attempting to cover with his coat sleeve.

As my mother and I walked through the parking lot, Jonathan and Walter were several feet behind. Jonathan asked Walter, "Is that a loner bracelet from the Mid-life Crisis Store?"

"Harmony bought it."

"Along with everything else, you two also had time to shop?"

"She's a go-getter."

"Unbelievable."

"What's unbelievable?"

"You ran across this woman yesterday, and she's got you going from ties to tie-dye. That's what's unbelievable."

"Love makes strange bedfellows."

"Which is one more thing I don't want to think about," Jonathan said.

A short time later, we cruised down State Street in Walter's Lincoln Town Car. My mother rode shotgun. Jonathan and I were in the back seat.

I peered into the glowing cafes and crowded bars as we traveled in a northwesterly direction, away from the shoreline. One and two-story establishments lined the quaint downtown street. The sidewalks were red brick pavers, laid in a basket-weave pattern, creating an atmosphere that was more village than city.

While we stopped at a traffic light, bass notes pumped from a crowded bar. Being overly tired, I assumed my eyes were playing tricks on me. I glanced at the bar and I swore the entire wedding party danced in a circle, clapping as a couple eerily resembling Florina and Cousin Cosmo were dancing. The woman was bent forward, and the man simulated a slap-that-ass motion with his hand. Disgusting. The light turned green, and the car continued. I shook myself awake. I reminded myself that a mind can imagine crazy things when stressed.

"Wally, have you considered an electric car?" my mother asked.

"I am now," Walter answered.

Jonathan clenched his teeth and shook his head.

My gleeful mother applauded. "Or one of those smart cars! Mother Earth would appreciate the eco-friendly gas mileage!"

Walter showed his openness to the idea by raising his brows, pushing his lower lip upward, and issuing a single nod.

"Smart car? Dad, you better first talk to somebody about life insurance," Jonathan suggested. "Or maybe Harmony already has."

"Jonathan!" I snapped. "No more binge-watching 48 Hours."

Jonathan's insinuation flew over her head, but she gave an enthusiastic thumbs-up to his suggestion to look into life insurance.

They arrived at the restaurant, and the hostess guided them to their table. It was a dark and trendy place with plenty of wood and deep cushioned seats. At the center of each table were multiple flickering candles in thick amber jars.

My mother studied Jonathan and me in the romantic light.

"What are you staring at?" I asked.

"You two look like you belong together."

"What does that mean?" Jonathan asked.

"Piper and I talked about this before. You know how dogs and their owners eventually start looking alike? I'm seeing that in you two."

Jonathan frowned. "Gee, thanks for the compliment. Am I the dog in this relationship?"

"Oh, no. I meant that when two are in love, they eventually take on some of the same traits, that's all."

I narrowed my eyes at my mother. "This wasn't amusing the first time you brought this up."

Jonathan knew better not to pursue my mother's thoughts further and instead studied the menu.

"I bought you a gift, Wally," my mother said. "I thought it would be fun to give it to you now." She reached into her handbag and pulled out a large T-shirt with a brightly colored spiral pattern splashed across the front, which Jonathan assumed was designed by a glitter-filled unicorn with morning sickness.

Jonathan couldn't believe his eyes. "That's for my dad?"

My jaw dropped. "To wear?"

"Of course, to wear. Wally will look adorable in it! He needs to update his look. Go ahead, Wally. Hold it up to your neck and let us have a look."

Walter laid the T-shirt across his torso and wrinkled his nose.

"Yeah, that's you, Dad," Jonathan mocked.

Walter laid the T-shirt across the back of his chair. "Thank you, Chipmunk." Then, in his best poker face, he said, "Can't wait to wear it."

She responded with a grin and little handclaps.

Jonathan furrowed his brow and scoffed like a camel who just received the last straw on his back—put there by my mother.

The waiter greeted them with menus. "I'll let you have a few minutes to decide. In the meantime, what can I get you to drink?"

Mother and I ordered wine, Walter ordered Scotch straight up, and Jonathan went with the unsweetened iced tea.

My mother's mouth turned crooked, and her eyes blinked upon hearing Jonathan's drink selection.

"What?" he asked.

"Iced tea? How exciting," she said sarcastically.

"If it helps you, think of it as the smart car of drinks."

Walter stood and announced his urge for a trip to the restroom.

"I better follow him," Jonathan said. "I need to make sure he doesn't end up at a poetry reading instead."

"A poetry reading! Cool! Where?" my mother asked, scanning the restaurant.

"He's joking, Mother."

Walter and Jonathan stood and headed for the restroom.

Jonathan's facial expression was one I'd never seen before. I was worried about him. My heart pounded at the thought of Jonathan confronting his father in the restroom and causing everything, including the wedding, to fall apart. "Excuse me, Mother. I have to use the restroom, too."

I hurried past both of them and pushed my way through the crowd of diners standing near the hostess station. The hostess mistook my panicked face for an urge to use the restroom and pointed around the corner. After dashing through the hallway, I paused at a door marked *MEN*. Placing my ear on the door, I listened for any signs of life in there: voices, flushing, zipping up, flatulence—nothing but silence. I pushed the door open, ran to a stall, and shut the door. I stood on the toilet because some genius designed every stall door in the world to stop short of reaching the floor. My high heels visible under the door might be a red flag.

Jonathan and Walter entered. I peeked over the top of the stall. Only the top of Walter's head was visible from my angle. He stood at what I guessed was a urinal while Jonathan waited by the sink. I peeked through the gap in the door at the sink area. Walter moved next to Jonathan at the twin sinks, and they washed their hands. Walter pulled his hands out from under the faucet water and waved one hand in front of the paper towel dispenser. No paper towel rolled out. Then he waved his hand again. Nothing. He added his other hand to the task and waved both over, under, and on each side of the dispenser. Nothing.

"There's a crank on the side," Jonathan said.

Walter turned the handle, and a paper towel rolled out the bottom of the dispenser. "Huh. Given the prices on the menu, they should have a guy here handing towels out."

So far, so good. Jonathan surprised me by remaining calm, though I was ready to open the stall door if push came to shove.

I moved to the hinge side of the door and peeked through the vertical gap. Jonathan stood in front of the mirror, brushing his hair with his fingers. He observed Walter in the reflection. "So, Dad. You doing okay? You feeling okay about things?"

I adjusted my position again and triggered the automatic toilet to flush.

From my restricted view through the crack, it appeared that Jonathan stooped down and searched under the stalls for feet. My heart raced.

He said to his dad, "Those things flush on their own sometimes."

Wow. I narrowly escaped having to explain why I'm standing on a toilet in the men's room.

Walter asked Jonathan, "What were you saying before? Am I feeling okay about things?"

"Dad, this new life of yours... Are you comfortable with everything? The new age bracelet, the lifestyle, your future smart car?"

"What are you getting at?"

Jonathan shrugged. "Seems like the old Walter is no longer." He pointed at Walter's new bracelet and said, "*This* is the new Walter. Are you okay with that?"

"I'm just trying to make her happy. I spent a lifetime putting myself first, so I'm trying something new. No doubt it all seems crazy to you, Son, but I'm in love. It makes little sense on paper, that's for sure, but I'm head over heels."

Awww. I must admit, that was kind of sweet.

Jonathan smiled as if he understood. "There's nothing wrong with being gaga for someone and wanting to please them. That's a good thing. But when it goes too far, and you totally lose who you are… well… there's a name for that—the first word starts with *p* and the second ends with *whipped*."

"What? I'm not whipped. That's not what's happening here. I'm my own man still.
You've got me all wrong. All wrong." Walter left the restroom. Jonathan followed him out.

I waited a minute to make sure they were all the way down the hallway.

When the coast was clear, I opened the stall door just as a male customer in a suit and tie entered. He spotted me and froze. His eyes widened. He jerked the door back open and angled his head to read the name *MEN*.

I had to think fast. I feigned confidence as I strode past him. I said, "Don't worry, I'm a man trapped in a woman's body."

The customer stared at me with his mouth open.

I hurried back to our table. Jonathan and Walter were just sitting down.

"Is everything cool?" my mother asked Walter.

Walter didn't respond.

I sat next to Jonathan.

Jonathan interjected with a baby voice. "Wally, Chipmunk asked you a question."

I dug my heel into the top of Jonathan's shoe.

Walter turned his head and searched the room. "Where's the damn waiter? I'd like to order something before the place closes."

My mother smiled. "Don't worry, Wally. I ordered for you."

"You what?"

"You were in the restroom when the waiter showed up. I thought it would be cute if I ordered for you. I want to start our marriage off healthy."

Jonathan smirked at Walter.

A waiter approached the table and asked Jonathan, "Can I take your order, sir? The lady here already ordered for everyone else when you were in the restroom."

"Oh, okay. I'll have a filet mignon. And a baked potato."

Walter chugged his Scotch.

A short while later, the waiter brought the food on a large tray to the table. He sat the tray on a stand, picked up the first plate, and said to Jonathan. "The filet mignon for you, sir. Careful with the plate; it's sizzling hot. And may I say, an excellent choice, sir. Excellent."

Next, he set my plate in front of me. Then he served my mother.

Finally, the waiter turned to Walter. He glanced at the T-shirt draped on the back of Walter's chair and smiled. "Fun shirt, by the way. And here, sir, is your delicious parsnip soup."

"My what?"

"Parsnip soup, Wally," my mother beamed. "With hazelnuts."

Walter pointed at Jonathan's expensive cut of meat and said, "But, but he's having—"

"Parsnip soup is what I ordered for you, sweetie," she said, cutting him off. "We have to eat healthy."

Jonathan was smiling and preparing his baked potato. He extended a small bowl of fluffy butter toward Walter. "Dad, *whipped*?"

"No," my mother answered for him. "Parsnip soup doesn't need butter."

Walter narrowed his eyes at Jonathan.

"What the hell is a parsnip, anyway?" Walter muttered.

"It's a root. Think of it like a carrot," I answered.

"Mind if I try *not* to think of it?" Walter said, staring longingly at Jonathan's steak.

My mother patted Walter's leg under the table. "Just try it, Wally. It'll grow on you."

"Then I'll try not to spill it."

The waiter approached our table again. "Is everything to your satisfaction?"

Walter pointed to Jonathan's plate. "I'll have what he's

having."

"Very good, sir." The waiter hurried off.

"Wally! I'm trying to teach you healthy habits. You agreed to be more open about things."

"Mother, he might need to transition into your lifestyle a little slower. I think he's doing pretty well so far. Let him have a little steak. The world's not going to end."

Walter pointed his parsnip soup spoon at me. "That's a smart woman, right there."

My mother sank in her chair. "Alright. I'll loosen the noose just a little. But not much. Wally, you said you'd make me happy."

Walter avoided eye contact with Jonathan and mumbled something inaudible.

"I can't hear you, Wallypog. What did you say?" my mother asked.

"I just wanted some tenderloin meat. I have to keep my strength up. Remember, I'm carrying you over the threshold tonight."

I winced. "TMI."

"What's that?" Walter asked.

"Too much information," my mother answered. She leaned on Walter. "But not too much for me. I like it when you get sexy."

"TMI, again," said Jonathan.

Walter kissed my mother on the cheek. "You're a lucky lady. I'm going to carry you over the threshold tonight at the hotel, out of tradition, and then again at home."

She sat up straight. "Home, as in Sausalito?"

Walter tilted his head at her. "The Bay Area? Ha! I don't think so. When I said *home*, I meant Bel Air, where I live."

"But I can't live in L.A. I have a store in Sausalito. Bohemian Bliss. The locals depend on me for their staples."

"You sell staples? Milk, meat, bread?" Walter asked.

"Of course not. Those aren't staples. I carry the essentials—candles, aromatherapy oils, and dream catchers."

Walter furrowed his brow. "I don't know what that is. Dream catcher?"

She shook her head. "Stop kidding."

"Mother, I don't think he knows."

She laughed. "Everyone knows what a dream catcher is."

"He doesn't," Johnathan said. "*I* barely know what it is."

"Okay, I'll play along," she said, still laughing at the notion of someone not having heard of an item that plays such an essential role in everyone's daily life. "It's a hoop, webbing, and feathers. It's used to catch dreams. Duh."

Walter twisted his body toward her. "Your customers are going to have to buy their dream catchers elsewhere. I'm not living in Sausalito."

She stiffened her back. "I'm not living in Bel Air."

They both stared straight ahead in silence.

Finally, she said, "Maybe we didn't think this through."

"I guess not."

Another awkward moment of silence passed.

"I'm not budging," she said.

"Me either," Walter responded. "I guess our impulsive marriage was a mistake."

More awkward silence.

"You'll work it out," I said. "Marriages are about compromises."

"I thought he loved me," she said to me.

"I do," Walter said.

"Then, Wally, our marriage wasn't a mistake."

They leaned toward each other and embraced.

She continued. "I love you so much. You're more important to me than my store."

"Are you saying you'll live in Bel Air? I hope you say *yes* because I won't move to the Bay Area. I'm putting my foot down on this one."

"Wally, I look forward to you carrying me across the threshold in my new home—in Bel Air."

They hugged again, and I clapped my hands.

Jonathan lifted his glass of unsweetened tea in the air. "Welcome back, Dad."

On the ride back to the hotel, they passed the same bar where I might have spotted our wedding party and a few of my crazy relatives. Police parked several squad cars in front of the bar. The blinding red and blue lights flashed across my face as I peered out the backseat window. I kept quiet. I didn't want to be the one to tell them our wedding party needed bailing out again. They always behead the messenger.

Walter glanced at the commotion. "Well, at least our wedding party and guests aren't the only ones in Santa Barbara causing trouble."

He turned on the radio to get more information.

From the car speakers, a voice said, "It looks like the storm we predicted to be gone by morning is now stalled just offshore. We have at least one more day of rain."

CHAPTER 17

The storm that stalled over the coastline, causing my wedding to be delayed another day, was too much for me to handle.

This. Can. Not. Be. Happening!

I had done all I could do to hold things together for a couple of days, but one more day might prove disastrous. The obstacles preventing me from being married were like a demon I thought I'd slain. I had placed my boot on his neck and raised my sword victoriously. And just when I finally exhaled, he bolted up again and clutched my ankle.

It was the middle of the night, and I resorted to the only thing left for me to do in this dark time of desperation—I called room service for snacks. Unfortunately, they had nothing to satisfy my binge-eating urge. They did point out that the trays of cake balls custom-made for my wedding reception were rapidly becoming stale.

After the cake balls were delivered to my room, I called Cassie to join me. We over-stuffed our faces with sugar and carbs, without any concern for tomorrow's bathroom scale results—as if a planet-destroying meteor was speeding toward Earth. What made matters worse was that the balls were decorated with either chocolate tuxedo frosting or white frosting to simulate a wedding dress, complete with tiny candy pearls. Despite the staleness, popping the frosted morsels into my mouth, one at a time, was both a delicious and torturous experience. Because these desserts were meant for the wedding reception, it broke my heart to devour them. I would gaze at each wedding-themed cake ball with great remorse, pop the whole tasty, spherical dessert into my mouth, and wail like a baby after swallowing it. Each bite was a reminder that my wedding was postponed yet again.

As I sobbed, Cassie patted my back and assured me of two things: first, the short delay shouldn't be the end of the world, and second, it would be a welcomed relief if I would order something to help wash the stale and dry cake balls down. Briefly setting aside the plausible idea that the world was ending, I ordered up some wedding reception champagne.

Cassie's taste preference shifted as the night progressed. At around 3 a.m., she switched from preferring chocolate tuxedo cake balls to vanilla frosted wedding dress cake balls. We sipped bottles of wedding reception champagne and discussed how pretty and sparkly the bottles were when viewed through our iPhone camera lenses—especially when the flash went off.

We were giggling and becoming more intoxicated by the minute. Cassie had an idea but couldn't stop laughing long enough to convey it to me. She finally calmed down enough to suggest that we take a photo of me in my wedding dress with a pillow strategically placed to make me look pregnant. I laughed, but shook my head. We were drunk, but not *that* drunk.

The more champagne we guzzled, the more cake balls we ate, and the more cake balls we ate, the more champagne we guzzled. A vicious circle that mercilessly ended when we passed out cold.

The morning had arrived, and Jonathan came to my room to escort me to the café on the first floor. I'm not sure why, but my legs were wobbly on the way to the elevator. Once inside, the doors closed, and I leaned against him while it descended to the first floor. He held me in his arms and stroked my hair as I pressed my swollen, teary, snotty face against his chest. I left a trace of slimy substance on the front of his shirt, and trying to wipe it away made a smeary mess. Jonathan lowered his head to see what I was doing and groaned. I lifted my eyes to offer an apologetic half-smile. My body was limp, almost lifeless, and I would have dropped to the elevator floor in a puddle of self-pity if Jonathan had not been standing there to hold me up.

Ding!

The cheery but pointless note pounded in my head as the elevator doors parted. A crowd of strangers milled about and had the audacity to be preoccupied with their own lives and their own vacations. They were happy, busy, bustling, shopping, laughing, dining, conversing, and otherwise astonishingly unaware that my wedding day plans had crashed overnight like a stack of wedding reception china during a California quake. My only thought was, *how dare they*? The least I expected from passersby at a time like this was an appropriate amount of sympathy. They went about their own lives, pretending to be oblivious to my predicament. Was a touch of solemnity too much to ask? Yes, children could still run about on the indoor pool deck, but was it necessary for them to laugh, scream, and giggle? None of the hotel guests I passed gave a damn about what I was going through. My wedding had been canceled again, and for some mysterious reason, the uncaring earth was still turning.

"It'll be okay," Jonathan said as he guided me through the resort's first floor.

Although my legs were moving, they moved reluctantly. I slipped on my oversized dark sunglasses to help avoid eye contact with anyone I might know. I wore a baseball cap with my ponytail poking through the opening in the back, and my I-don't-care-anymore pink fuzzy slippers. My brain throbbed, and my stomach ached.

Jonathan helped ease me into a chair in the hotel café.

A server asked what we'd like to order.

"I think she'll just have coffee," Jonathan guessed. "Is that right, honey?"

I sat slumped over and held up my index finger to indicate my answer was *yes*.

Howie approached our table. "Good morning, guys. Hey, I haven't seen Cassie yet. Is she coming down to breakfast?"

I didn't move. I remained slumped over and held up the same index finger to indicate my answer—and this time, somehow, it meant *no*.

"Why are you looking for Cassie?" Jonathan asked.

Howie wasn't ready for that probing question, and he had no reason, other than his sophomoric crush, to be asking for Cassie. He ad-libbed. "I wanted to go over our parts in the wedding. It was moved to tomorrow, right?"

Jonathan shook his head in an effort to stop Howie from pursuing any more questions concerning schedules.

Howie's idea of changing the subject was to ask, "Is this rain ever going to end?"

Still not looking up, I held up my index finger again to indicate my answer—this time, it meant *who knows?*

"Okay, I'll leave you two lovebirds alone," Howie said as he turned to leave. Then he spun back around. "Oh, by the way, Piper, why were thirty-seven photos of empty champagne bottles texted to me in the middle of the night?"

I sat up on that one and squinted at him. "What?"

"Yeah. Some from you, some from Cassie."

Jonathan checked his phone's text messages. "Me too."

I closed my eyes and groaned.

I scanned the café and spotted a few from my wedding party, along with a few of my mother's guests. About half were showing their phone screens to someone else. From my vantage point, the photos were blurry, but there was no doubt they were showing each other low-quality photos of empty champagne bottles.

"What was that all about?" Jonathan asked.

I said, "Give me time—I'll come up with a reason that makes sense."

"You were drunk texting?" Jonathan asked, horrified at the thought.

"Actually, there's no *text* on her messages. Just photos," Howie said.

Jonathan asked, "Howie, can you please do me a favor? Take a walk and see if anyone from Hyde's office is snooping around."

"Are you trying to get rid of me?"

"Yes."

"Alright. I get it." Before he left, he laughed as he said, "That one photo was funny, Piper."

My eyes widened.

Howie continued. "Just so you know—" He interrupted himself by laughing again. "Stuffing seven cake balls in your cheeks at once is not a world record." Howie turned to leave, but stopped again. He viewed his phone and laughed.

"Is it another photo?" I asked, dreading his answer.

"No," Howie answered. "It's not a photo from you."

I exhaled. A relieved expression formed on Jonathan's face too.

Howie said, "It's a video. From Cassie."

Howie returned to our table and pointed his screen at us. He pushed play.

The video featured me turned sideways in my wedding dress. The pillow under my dress made me look nine months pregnant. I giggled at the camera and said, "Jonathan, baby. I'm at the Elvis Wedding Chapel. Take responsibility for once. Make an honest woman out of me. Let's not raise a little bastard child." Then I lost balance and fell out of the frame.

"That went out to everyone," Howie said, laughing while he turned to leave.

Jonathan swiped through Cassie's text messages on his phone. He stopped when he reached the late-night photos of empty champagne bottles and the pregnant bride video.

Burying my face in my hands, I said, "I don't remember doing that. I really don't."

Jonathan pinched the bridge of his nose with his thumb and index finger. "Honey…"

I braced myself. When Jonathan started a sentence with the word *honey*, what followed was usually something a person would never say to their honey.

"I'm running for Congress. Drunk texting and joking around

like that is something that could ruin my career overnight. This is sensitive stuff. There are forces out there that will turn the smallest, most innocent thing into a national scandal."

My entire body cringed. "I know, I know. I'm sorry. I'm afraid I was trying to find out what drowns sadness and frustration best—sugary treats or champagne. Champagne won."

The hotel's restaurant manager approached me. He was a middle-aged wiry man who wore a suit, a tie, and a frown. "Excuse me, ma'am."

I was completely and utterly exhausted and barely lifted my head up to speak. "Yes?"

He pointed at my feet.

"What?" I asked.

He cleared his throat. "I must inform you we have a dress code here at The Oceanfront Hotel, and that code specifically states that only appropriate attire shall be worn in the restaurants. If you'd like to view the list of acceptable apparel, it's on our website. Until there's an amendment to the rules, you'll have to change your pink fuzzy slippers."

I sat up straight. My blood must have reached the boiling point. I stood up and walked around the table until I was face to face with him.

"Slippers?" I said. "You're bothered by my pink fuzzy slippers?"

"My job is to enforce the rules."

I grabbed his tie and pulled him closer. "Now you listen to me and you listen good. I've not only had a bad day, I've had three bad days before this one. I've had lousy weather that, so far, has cost me two more nights times twelve rooms in your overpriced hotel. Not to mention a private detective photographing my wedding rehearsal."

"A private what?" Jonathan asked.

I froze for a second. Then I lowered my voice to Jonathan. "Well, it could've happened. Who knows?"

The restaurant manager's eyes grew wider.

I continued. "We've had to bail-out relatives and the wedding party from jail—twice. I've got a soon-to-be father-in-law who was born angry, a crazy mother, and crazier relatives. And a wedding site on the beach that's been blown to Nevada—"

"Piper! Get a hold of yourself," Jonathan said. He was next to me, trying to pry my hands off the restaurant manager's tie.

I lost control of myself and was unaware of my actions. My eyes moved to the tie I was gripping. I let go and glanced around to get my bearings. I began to cry. "I'm so sorry," I said to the restaurant manager, straightening the wrinkles from his tie. "I don't know what's come over me. Please forgive me."

Jonathan put his arms around me and sat me down.

"Okay, lady, you can wear the fuzzy slippers," the restaurant manager said, his eyes still full of fear.

I apologized again. "Please understand. I'm under the influence of cake balls and champagne. I don't know what I'm doing." I began to hyperventilate as I questioned my own sanity. Am I one of those crazed brides I've always made fun of?

The restaurant manager extended his palms toward me as he backed away. "Let's… just… pretend this whole thing never happened."

"I can't say I'm sorry enough," I said.

He left the dining area and hurried through the swinging kitchen doors.

I faced Jonathan and said, "I'm so sorry to you too. Do you still want to marry me?"

He tried to force a smile. "Yes, I still want to marry you. We just need to get everything back under control."

"Okay. I just need to calm down." I leaned on him and took a deep breath.

Howie hurried back to their table. "Jonathan, you need to follow me."

"Not now."

"This is urgent."

"Is it another Snickers hung up in the vending machine? Just bang on the glass."

Howie crossed his arms and glared at Jonathan.

"Alright, alright," Jonathan said.

CHAPTER 17

I wanted to lay my head on the table and close my eyes as they walked away, but something inside told me to go with them. Something was wrong, and I needed to be there. Besides, things couldn't get worse. Right?

CHAPTER 18

I caught up to them as we stepped outside the hotel doors. The rainfall was heavy. Howie popped open an umbrella and handed a similar one to Jonathan. Each umbrella prominently displayed the hotel's logo. Jonathan pulled me close to him so that his umbrella would keep me dry.

A white-bearded man paced back and forth in the rain on the city sidewalk with a picket sign.

"There he is," Howie said, pointing at the protester.

"What about him?" Jonathan asked.

Howie grabbed Jonathan's arm and pulled him closer to the protester. "See?"

The white-bearded man was clutching onto a stick attached to a poster-sized sign. He held the soggy sign high enough for passing vehicles to see. On the sign was a photo of Jonathan's face in a red circle with a diagonal line. In bold letters above the photo were the words "Jonathan Knight is a pervert!"

We marched across the lawn toward the protester.

When we reached the sidewalk, Jonathan handed me the umbrella and walked alongside the man.

My head was pounding, so I stood back and watched.

Jonathan asked the protestor, "What's this about?"

The protester ignored Jonathan and continued walking.

"Hey, dude!" Howie yelled at the man. "What's your problem?"

The protester stopped and pointed to his sign. "It's about that guy." Then he resumed walking.

Jonathan and Howie were on either side of the protester,

keeping up with him stride for stride.

"Why do you think he's a perv?" Howie asked.

"I got no comment," the white-bearded man replied.

Jonathan stepped in front of the man, stopping him. "Well, your sign is certainly a comment. Care to elaborate?"

The man angled his eyes up at his sign. Then he faced Jonathan. "Here's my comment then. Jonathan Knight—" He stopped once again and read his sign as a refresher course, "…is a pree-vert."

Howie rolled his eyes. "It doesn't say *pree-vert*—it says *pervert*. As in *Jonathan Knight's a pervert.*"

"Howie!" Jonathan admonished.

"Right." Howie turned to the protestor. "Jonathan Knight is neither of those things."

The protester stepped around Jonathan and continued walking.

Jonathan kept right beside him. "I must inform you that your sign is defamatory, and you can be sued. The right to free speech does not include the right to slander."

"The man who hired me said that as long as it's true, I can't be sued."

Jonathan and Howie both uttered, "Malcolm Hyde."

The driver of a passing car rolled the window down, slowed, read the sign, and yelled, "Another sick bastard! I won't be voting for him!" The man drove away.

Howie pulled his wallet out of his back pocket. "How much did Hyde pay you to do this?"

Jonathan waved off Howie. "I'm innocent. I'm not paying anyone to go away."

A police car came to a stop at the curb. The officer pulled the hood of his raincoat over his head and approached the three men. "What's going on, fellas?"

Howie said, "This man is slandering my friend."

"That so?" asked the policeman. Then his eyes widened. "Hey, you're Jonathan Knight. Why are you out here protesting yourself?"

"I'm not protesting. I'm a guest at this hotel. I'm trying to get this guy to go away."

"Officer," I shouted. "I can vouch for Jonathan. He's not a pervert! I've known him for a couple of months." As soon as the words left my lips, I knew that didn't help matters.

The protester studied Jonathan. Then he checked his sign. Then turned back again toward Jonathan. "You're Jonathan Knight?"

Jonathan faced the policeman. "Officer, can you tell him to move along?"

"I'd like to, but I'm afraid there's nothing I can do about it."

The policeman returned to his car and drove away, leaving Jonathan and Howie to fend for themselves.

The protester resumed his pacing while Jonathan and Howie followed close behind.

"How much did Hyde pay you?" Howie demanded to know.

"Howie! Stop," Jonathan shouted.

Howie tried again. "How much?"

"Fifty bucks," answered the protester.

"I'll give you fifty-one to go away," Howie said.

The protester stopped and stroked his long white beard while considering the deal. "Naw. Better not. They paid me to do a job, and dammit, I'm going to do it and do it well. I'm a man of principles."

"Just my luck," Jonathan said. "A homeless man with a work ethic."

Howie was determined. "How 'bout I throw in money for a Filet-O-Fish sandwich?"

"Deal!" The protester threw his sign down, took the money from Howie, and walked in the direction of the nearest McDonald's.

Howie picked up the sign, broke the stick off, and tossed it down. The sign flipped over in the wind and tumbled away in the storm. Howie caught up with Jonathan, and we all returned to the hotel.

"It's getting ugly, isn't it?" Jonathan asked.

"Yep. You're climbing in the polls. He'll stop at nothing."

By noon, the sun finally broke through the clouds, and the wind diminished to nothing more than a typical ocean breeze. Unfortunately, the break in the weather came too late to undo that day's cancelation of the wedding ceremony. I hired a crew to restore the site on the beach where the wedding would take place. They replaced the large floral arch and cleared the sand of seaweed and debris from the storm. They brought folding chairs back and placed them before the arch, leaving a gap down the center of the chairs to form an aisle.

After a much-needed nap, I regained most of my energy, which allowed me to oversee the restoration of the wedding site. I was finally feeling stronger, not only physically, but emotionally. Restoring the wedding site made my cares quickly disappear like cake balls off a tray at 3 am. In a little more than twenty-four hours, I'd be married. My heart beat faster just thinking about it.

The scene played out in my mind. Jonathan and I would face our seated guests as Brother Larry introduced us as Mr. and Mrs. Knight. We would then walk back down the aisle together, starting our life as a married couple. And Jonathan wouldn't mind that I made him go through the ceremony without shoes, or so I hoped.

Then I admitted to myself that maybe I was a tad too unrealistic. I rephrased that last sentence in my mind. *And I didn't mind that Jonathan refused to go barefoot during the ceremony.*

Yep, that was more realistic. And I was okay with that. Being married to him was all that really mattered.

I smiled, tilted my head back, and let the sunshine warm my face. My life was back on course and heading straight for that happy ending. Or, more accurately stated, that happy beginning. Finally, all was well.

A noise invaded my thoughts. A noise that wasn't a part of the wedding site restoration. Grumbling, mumbling, a few choice curse words, and heavy breathing interrupted my daydream. I turned around to see none other than Malcolm Hyde trudging through the sand. The white-bearded protester and Griggs, wearing his blue Dodger cap, accompanied Hyde.

The two were carrying a podium displaying a congressional seal. They placed it upright in the sand near the wedding site.

I hurried toward the podium and the three men. I stopped just a few feet away from Hyde.

He held his hand out to shake mine. "Afternoon, ma'am. I'm always happy to meet and shake the hand of one of my constituents."

I ignored his offer to shake hands.

"You're Malcolm Hyde. What are you doing here?"

Hyde said, "I recognized you from the surveillance photos." His eyebrows and his mouth turned downward. "You must be the fiancé of my opponent."

"This is our wedding site," I said. "Please take your podium and whatever else you're planning and move it elsewhere."

Hyde responded with a hearty laugh. "I'd suggest you run along, little girl. You're interfering with the people's business. The people of the twenty-fourth Congressional District, I should add."

"What the hell are you talking about? This is my wedding site, and you need to leave immediately!"

Hyde surveyed the site and smiled. "I appreciate you going through all this work because the only thing this site will be used for is my victory party after my big win in a few months. That is, if another storm doesn't blow it away by then." He laughed again.

I folded my arms and stood my ground. I wasn't going to let Hyde or his henchmen invade my territory.

A few more people arrived and stood near the podium. After a few minutes, others came and joined the growing crowd.

I needed to let Jonathan know what was happening. I reached into my pocket for my mobile phone, but I had left it under a tray of half-eaten cake balls.

Several local TV news vans arrived. Reporters and their crews lugged cameras and sound equipment across the sand to the podium. Several more people joined the growing crowd, and a few who happened to be strolling near the waves hurried over.

A female reporter in a yellow blazer held a small hand mirror and ran a tube of lipstick across her lips in preparation for her live shot. A camera operator focused his lens on her face, and another crew member donned headphones and adjusted dials in an audio bag. She faced the camera and spoke into her microphone. "I'm Jessica Picante. We have some breaking news from Santa Barbara. Congressman Malcolm Hyde is about to hold a live press conference right here on the sand. As you can see behind me, a podium has been set up. Any minute now, Congressman Hyde will address the media about information he's obtained he calls a *bombshell*." She glanced behind her. "Oh. The congressman is stepping to the microphones now. Let's listen in."

Hyde smiled and cleared his throat. He straightened his tie and ran his palm over his slicked-down hair to ensure the breeze hadn't ruffled a strand. He tapped on the microphone several times. "Thank you, everyone, for attending this last-minute press conference. There are times in a public servant's career when he—or she—comes across disturbing facts. For me, this morning was one of those times. I happened to be driving to the Salvation Army headquarters to drop off clothing, food, and whatever money I could for the underprivileged here in the Twenty-fourth Congressional District. My route happened to take me right by this hotel. That's when a crowd of protesters appeared on the sidewalk."

That appeared to stun the white-bearded man who searched around for the crowd he couldn't remember.

Hyde continued. "I'm telling you, my friends, they were angry. Anytime constituents of mine aren't happy, I do my best to find out what the problem is so that I can solve it. I slowed down and read the signs they carried. There were even a few photos on the signs."

"Get to the point!" a reporter shouted.

Hyde ignored the request. "One of the protesters walked over to my car window and filled me in. Now, let me preface what I'm about to say with this: I'm a family man and believe that families are the bedrock foundation of our society. In my years of legislating, I've done everything I could to bolster the family unit."

"Get to the bombshell you promised!" another reporter shouted.

"As I was saying," Hyde droned on. "There's nothing wrong with close families. Nothing at all. But there's a point I draw the line. A line my opponent doesn't mind crossing."

"Please, sir. We're carrying this live," Jessica Picante pleaded. "Cut to the chase."

"After the protesters begged me to do something, I returned to my office immediately to verify the facts. And I'm sorry to report that my opponent, Jonathan Knight, has decided to marry his…" Hyde paused and wiped his forehead with a handkerchief for dramatic effect. Then he finished his sentence. "…stepsister."

The reporters, their crews, and a few others who gathered on the beach gasped.

"And that spot there," Hyde pointed to my weddings site, "is the very site they'll join together something that should never be joined together."

Most of the reporters scampered to the wedding arch and snapped a barrage of photos.

"And if you'd like a comment from my opponent's fiancé—or should I say stepsister—there she is." Hyde pointed at me.

The reporters rushed toward me. They shoved microphones in my face and shouted a thousand questions at once. The chaotic sound of the crazed mob filled my ears. I tried to back away, but the reporters surrounded me.

"Is it true?" they shouted.

"We just met," I answered. "We're not blood relatives. We're just like any other couple!"

A reporter shouted, "Are you in love with your stepbrother?"

"Does this end Jonathan Knight's campaign?" another asked.

The mob pushed me until I bumped into Jessica Picante, who was in the middle of wrapping it up and speaking into her mic. "Well, there you have it. You heard it first-hand. If true, Jonathan Hyde has some explaining to do. I'm Jessica Picante. Back to you in the studio."

I glanced at Hyde. He was grinning at the chaotic scene.

I pushed my way through the throng of reporters and hurried back to the hotel as several attempted to follow me.

I tried my best not to cry, but tears streamed down my cheeks. I was becoming sick to my stomach.

CHAPTER 19

I cried uncontrollably and ran through the hotel lobby. Instead of stopping at the elevators, I used the stairs to climb the seven stories to my suite. I had to avoid being caught in an elevator with happy guests who would only wonder why they were sharing a confined space with a sobbing, hysterical, possibly dangerous woman who had either taken an excessive dose of medication or was in desperate need of an excessive dose of medication.

I pushed open the seventh-floor stairwell door and hurried through the hallway toward my suite.

"Piper?" Cassie asked. "What's wrong?"

I was so focused on getting to my hotel room, I wasn't aware I ran past Cassie. I was frantic and reached the door of my room, swiping the room key card several times before the door opened. Cassie followed me in. I ran to the suite's bedroom and collapsed on the bed. Then I rolled over, face up, covered my head with a pillow, and continued to cry.

"What happened?" Cassie asked.

I kept the pillow covering my head with one arm, and with the other arm, I pointed several times in no particular direction.

"What? What are you saying?" Cassie persisted.

I pointed several more times until my arm collapsed at my side.

"That's not telling me anything. Piper, you need to tell me why you're crying. Is it something Jonathan said?"

I waved off the question.

"Is it something he did?"

I continued to sob while my hand made a dismissive motion.

"Is it something your mother said?"

The same dismissive hand motion served as an answer.

"Is it something your mother *did*?"

A big thumbs up on that one.

Cassie removed the pillow covering my head. I kept my eyes shut tight. My face was hot and must have been blood red. Tears streamed down my cheeks.

"What did your mother do?"

Between gagging on sobs and gasping for air, I said, "She m-m-married my f-f-f-fiancé's f-f-father."

"I know that. We've known that since yesterday. Why the sudden hysteria *now*?"

I didn't have the strength to elaborate. I had just enough energy to wonder what the criminal sentencing guidelines would be for someone found guilty of strangling their mother with the vines from a floral wedding arch.

I sat halfway up, pointed at the balcony, then collapsed back onto the bed.

Cassie walked to the glass door, opened it, and stepped onto the balcony. She scanned the deck but found nothing out of the ordinary. She returned to the bedroom. "Piper, there's nothing on the balcony. I don't know what you want me to see."

I swung my legs to the floor and walked to the balcony while clutching a pillow. While sobbing, I pointed to the beach below.

Cassie bent over the railing and scanned the beach. A crowd mulled around the wedding arch. A few steps away, Hyde was waving his arms and speaking to a group that appeared to be interested in whatever he was saying.

"Hyde's down there. What's going on? Does it have anything to do with you?"

I lifted the pillow to my head and buried my face in it while giving another thumbs up.

"Piper, you've got to sit up and talk. This is me, Cassie, you're dealing with here. Your college roommate who always finished last at charades."

I collapsed on the sofa and pointed to the TV.

Cassie picked up the remote control and pushed *power*.

On the screen were the words BREAKING NEWS. A blonde news anchor said, "We interrupt our regularly scheduled program for this breaking news. Congressman Malcolm Hyde wrapped up his press conference just a few minutes ago. He's claiming that his opponent, Jonathan Knight, the so-called common-sense candidate, is about to marry his stepsister. In the studio with us is our legal contributor. Sir, since this is your field of expertise, let me ask you this. Is marrying your stepsister legal in California?"

The legal expert pushed his glasses off the end of his nose and closer to his face. "Actually, there are no laws in the country against marrying a step-sibling. Two people with no common parents aren't related by blood, so the state allows them to marry."

I removed the pillow from my face and sat up.

"See?" Cassie said to me. "I hope that makes you feel better."

The legal expert added, "So, it *is* legal, but considered by many to be highly distasteful."

I fell back onto the sofa with the pillow over my head.

Cassie grimaced and muted the channel.

Someone knocked on the door.

Cassie went to the door, put her ear against it, and asked, "Who is it?"

"Jonathan."

She opened the door and let him in. "I'm glad you're here."

After a moment of silence, he said, "What is she doing?"

"Mainly pointing at stuff," Cassie answered.

Jonathan sat down next to me on the sofa. He wrapped his arm around me and helped me sit up. I leaned into him, and he cradled me in his arms.

"Baby, what's wrong?" he asked gently.

My tears continued to flow, and I formed a pout with my mouth, weeping silently.

"Wedding nerves?"

I cried harder.

He kissed my forehead and brushed my hair from my face with his fingers. "Don't be sad. We've been through the worst of it. Everything's fine now. We'll marry tomorrow, and all this stress will be a memory."

The TV station broke in with more news on the Congressman's press conference, and Cassie unmuted the sound.

Jonathan continued to speak soft and encouraging words. "Everything's alright. Don't cry. You're in my arms now." He glanced at the news update. "What the?" He stood abruptly, causing me to roll off him and tumble onto the floor. "Oh, God," he said, staring at the TV. "What's this about?"

I sat crossed legged on the floor with my head in my hands. Then I managed to squeak out a reply. "Hyde held a press conference. He announced to the world that you were marrying your… your…"

"Stepsister," Cassie said, completing my sentence.

Jonathan's breathing quickened. "How the hell did Hyde find out about this? This is not good. Not good at all." He paced the floor. "See, Piper? This is all because your mother couldn't keep her hands off my dad. Now look at the trouble we're in."

"It takes two to tango," I said.

He pointed an angry finger at me. Then stopped himself. "You're right. You're absolutely right. I agree. It's my dad's fault too." He continued to pace the floor, muttering. "I'd take him to the end of the pier and push him off, but he's probably wearing his new tie-dye T-shirt. Someone would spot those neon colors and rescue him immediately." He stopped pacing. "I need to get Howie in here."

Within minutes, Howie was at the door. Cassie let him in. Howie asked, "What's going on?"

Jonathan said, "Hyde told the press I was marrying my step—"

"Don't say it," I cut in.

Howie's eyes darted back and forth while he processed the

info. "Okay. Okay. I know what to do."

"You do?" Jonathan asked while resuming his pacing.

Howie began pacing too and ran into Jonathan.

Jonathan pushed him away.

"Sorry. My bad," Howie said.

"What's your idea, Howie?" Cassie asked. She gazed admiringly at Howie.

I did a double take at Cassie.

Howie said, "We need to form one of those war rooms. You know, a place for strategy sessions. That's what politicians do when they're caught doing something wrong."

"We didn't do anything wrong," I said.

"A war room? That's a little over the top," Jonathan said.

"This entire scenario is over the top."

"Howie's right," Cassie said. "We need to strategize."

Jonathan turned to Howie. "How did you come up with this war room idea?"

"Netflix."

Jonathan said he needed Howie to stay enthused and motivated, so they had their war room up and running in no time.

Howie shut the curtains, dimmed the lights, and lit a cigar. Jonathan and Howie paced the floor.

Cassie grabbed a bottle of wine and two glasses. She sat next to me on the sofa, encouraging me to take big sips.

Jonathan glanced at me and Cassie. "So, the first thing we need to figure out is how did Malcom Hyde find out about Harmony and my dad. We were all sworn to silence." He turned to Howie. "You didn't tell anyone, did you?"

"I didn't breathe a word. Wait. I did tell a friend," Howie admitted.

"Howie! Who did you tell?"

Howie held his hands out, palms down, in a let's-all-keep-cool gesture. "Don't worry. I was drinking at the hotel bar. I vaguely remember mentioning something about it, but it's cool. The guy didn't care."

"What guy?"

"You might have seen him around the hotel. He wears a Dodger cap. Don't worry; he's my new friend."

I sank lower into the sofa and took a huge swig of wine.

Howie was fortunate that he wasn't standing on Jonathan's imaginary pier. Jonathan would have shoved him off, too.

"You spoke to Hyde's man, I'm sure of it. He's probably a private detective or a campaign operative. You couldn't see that?"

"No, he's not that at all. He's a nature photographer."

Jonathan put his palm to his forehead. "And why would you think that?"

"His telephoto lens," Howie said, jiggling his head confidently. He shot Cassie a cocky smile.

Cassie's eyes widened, and she swallowed hard. Howie, pleased with her reaction, curled his lips into a slight smile.

Jonathan dropped back onto the sofa next to me and rubbed his forehead. He always does that when he's bracing himself for an impending migraine. He muttered, "Lord, give me the patience to not toss him out the window right now."

"We're on the seventh floor," I reminded him.

"I know. We're not high enough. He might survive."

Howie scratched his scalp. "Are you saying he might not be a nature photog—" Howie froze mid-sentence. He narrowed his eyes and gritted his teeth. "That lyin' sack. Diabolical!"

Jonathan stood up again. "What's done is done. Let's just move on."

There was another knock. Jonathan tip-toed to the door. He lowered his voice and asked, "Who is it?"

"Harmony."

Howie turned to us and held his hand up. "This could be a trick."

"Just open the door," I said.

He opened it, and my mother and Walter entered.

Walter's attire appeared to be back to normal except for the sandals. Yes, Walter was back to being himself, but not all the way back.

My mother's eyes scanned the darkened room until she found me. "What's wrong, sweetie?" she asked. "You've been crying."

I dabbed my eyes with a tissue. "The world just ended. Didn't you notice?"

"Not really." My mother flashed Walter a coy look. "Recently, I *did* feel the earth move. Or whatever that expression is. Right, Wallypog?"

Walter winked.

"Please, Mother. Gross. I'm being serious here."

My mother surveyed the mood of the others and said, "There's a heavy vibe in here. Before you tell me what's wrong, will a glass of wine help me?"

"An entire vineyard might not be enough." I answered.

My mother scanned the room. "You need some sunlight and fresh air in here."

Walter motioned for my mother to sit next to him. Instead, he opened the sliding glass door. She reached for Walter's hand and coaxed him out onto the balcony.

"Stay away from the window! Don't go out there!" Jonathan shouted.

She scoffed at his demand. "And why not?"

"The media. Down below. If they spot you, who knows what they'll think is going on in this room," Jonathan said.

My mother closed the glass door. "Okay, guys, what's going on?"

I took a deep breath. "In a press conference, Hyde announced Jonathan and I are…" I pointed to Cassie again to finish my sentence.

"Step-siblings," Cassie said.

I collapsed into Jonathan.

My mother laughed, waving off any concern.

"It's not funny, Mother. Jonathan will probably lose the election now. But worse…" I turned to Jonathan, "he probably wants to cancel the wedding." I buried my face in my hands and sobbed.

Jonathan turned to Howie. "We need to strategize."

"This is our war room," Howie said to my mother and Walter.

"Son, just ignore Hyde. It'll all go away," Walter said.

Jonathan shook his head. "It won't go away. My political career is in a death spiral."

"I'll go down and see if the hotel has any push pins and yarn," Howie said.

"If they have what?" I asked.

"Push pins and yarn." Howie then pointed. "We'll use this wall."

"What are you talking about?"

"It's what they do in movies—a big wall showing how things are linked together. Yarn going from one pushpin to another, connecting things like suspects, locations, and evidence."

"Howie, no crime has been committed," I said.

"But a big wall with all those strings looks cool. It's what you'd expect to see in a war room."

Jonathan shook his head. "We'll put three pushpins on the wall, and the yarn will link Howie's photo to the Dodger hat and the Dodger hat to the press conference. Case solved."

"Never mind," Howie said.

Jonathan walked past Howie, patting him on the shoulder. "Good thinking," he said sarcastically.

"It's all I could come up with," Howie said.

"Maybe instead of the pushpins and yarn idea, you should've advised me *yesterday* that we needed to get out in front of this story. That's what the pros do. *We* should have broken the bad news to the public." As Jonathan said that, he glanced at me.

"Bad news?" I asked. "So, you and I getting married is bad news."

"I said bad news? I meant odd news—wait—strange news." He threw his hands up in exasperation. "Let's not kid ourselves. It's bad news. Real bad news."

I stood up and put my hands on my hips. "You want to call off the wedding, don't you?"

"Did *I* say that? No. I didn't. I just meant that when something like this crops up, it's a good idea to be the first to shape how the public perceives it."

"Oh, brother," I sighed.

"There's that expression again. Please stop saying that. Hyde will turn it into my official campaign slogan."

"You should hold your own press conference," Cassie said.

Howie snapped his fingers. "I was just going to say that."

Jonathan walked to the edge of the sliding glass door and peeked down at the beach. "A press conference is risky. Maybe Dad is right—we should just ignore this whole thing."

"I think we should explain what happened," I said. "A press conference could explain how two normal people met, fell in love, but had no idea about their abnormal parents." I pointed at my mother and Walter.

Walter frowned. "Abnormal?"

My mother smiled. "Abnormal? I like it."

Jonathan squinted at the beach below. I walked to the sliding glass door and also peeked out.

The crowd at the wedding site was growing. A dozen or more people arrived carrying signs. They marched back and forth in front of the wedding arch. Jonathan squinted to read their signs, but the distance was too great. Several more TV news vans arrived, each with a reporter and crew.

"This is crazy. Hyde has apparently paid people to demonstrate in front of our wedding site," Jonathan said.

"What?" I asked.

My mother opened the sliding glass door and walked onto the balcony.

"Be careful," Jonathan warned. "Don't let them see you."

She ignored his warning.

"Harmony, come back in," Jonathan insisted.

"No one knows who I am. Besides, we're too far up. They can't see us."

Walter joined her on the balcony.

"I've lost control," Jonathan said.

"I have a hard time believing that crowd down there cares this much about our circumstance," I said.

"They don't," Jonathan said. "I'm sure they're on Hyde's payroll. The trouble is—a crowd attracts the media, and the media coverage attracts a bigger crowd. This could get out of control."

Jonathan picked up the remote control and flipped through the channels. Most featured news reporters standing on the beach.

"You have no choice," I said. "You'll have to hold a news conference and explain our situation. I'm sure people will understand." I pointed at my mother and Walter. "Their marriage was beyond our control. And apparently beyond theirs, too."

Everyone agreed that standing around and worrying wasn't helping, so they all sprang into action. Jonathan strategized while constantly monitoring the news channels. I opened a laptop computer and searched for an alternate wedding venue. My mother poured two glasses of wine and suggested Walter join her for some much-needed relaxation on the balcony lounge chairs. Cassie did her part to help by removing Howie from the war room and occupying his mind with a simple lunch in the hotel café.

The local news channel continually streamed live the chaotic scene on the beach. More angry people arrived carrying slanderous signs. Reporters interviewed anyone willing to give an opinion.

Two men grabbed the wedding arch and dragged it around the sand. "Sick bastards!" one of them shouted. "No step-siblings are gonna marry in my town!" They both ripped the wedding arch to pieces.

"Piper, there goes your wedding arch," my mother said between sips of wine from the lounge chair.

I ran onto the balcony and scanned the beach. Two men were tearing at the floral ornament. "Oh hell no!"

I turned and ran toward the door.

Jonathan grabbed my arm and pulled me away from the door.

"Where are you going?"

"I can put up with a lot of crap going on out there; I really can! But they crossed the line! You don't mess with a bride's wedding arch and live to tell about it!"

"Whoa! Whoa," Jonathan said. "We can get another one. You can't go down there with all those reporters. There are way too many cameras, and we don't need any more breaking news stories."

I broke free from his grasp and made a dash for the door. He matched me step for step. As we reached the door, he held his hand firmly against it, preventing me from pulling it open.

"Please, honey. Don't do it."

"Back away, Jonathan!"

"You'll only make matters worse. Just take some deep breaths."

After a few more tugs at the doorknob, I finally let go and took a step back.

"Thank you," he said. "I promise you we'll replace the arch. Those two idiots down there are no match for a bride-to-be. They're not worth the hard time you'll do in prison."

I shrugged my shoulders.

Jonathan continued. "Besides, visiting hours at San Quentin conflict with my golf schedule."

I turned my face away from his and tried to remain angry, but my lips couldn't help but form a slight smile. "I'm a defense attorney. I can get myself off."

"You have your hands full already with The Naked Strangler case."

My shoulders slumped, and I said, "Ugghh, he's guilty as sin, anyway. I'm not going to worry about him right now."

He hugged me and stroked my hair with his hand. "Please, just watch things from the balcony. Let's not be part of that craziness down there."

My anger was slowly dissipating, but being asked to view the beachfront chaos from the balcony wasn't helping. I loved and trusted Jonathan and agreed to abide by his wishes. Still, this situation had turned me into a typical bridezilla, and I briefly considered asking room service to deliver a bullhorn, grenades, binoculars, and an accurate sniper rifle.

CHAPTER 20

Jonathan convinced me to sit with him on the sofa and try to calm down.

I turned on the TV to take our minds off our problems for a few minutes.

The local news was still broadcasting live from the hotel's beach. On the screen, a family of backwoods hillbillies walked across the beach toward the wedding site—a father, mother, and five children.

I switched the channel.

Jonathan grabbed the remote. "Wait! What was that?" He turned back to the local news channel.

The hillbillies on the beach all had bright red hair and wore ragged, dirty, worn clothing. They approached a female reporter, Jessica Picante, who was in the middle of a live interview with a protester.

The hillbilly father interrupted the interview. "Wanna hear *my* two cents?"

Jessica stopped her interview, forced a smile, and turned toward the camera. "It seems we have someone here who wants to give his opinion."

"Yer right. I got plenty to say," the hillbilly father said.

He reached out and tugged on the microphone, but she wrestled it back. After composing herself, she asked the hillbilly father, "Sir, what's your take on the Jonathan Knight scandal?"

"Scandal?" He shook his head and laughed. "Now that's the part I just don't get. Me and the misses here was listening to all the fuss on the radio whilst we was soakin' up some vacation sun on that beach over yonder."

"Sir, I take it you're not from here?"

"Here? Naw. We're from Flattsville. If ya ain't furmiliar with Sorgum County, Flattsville's a stone's throw from Gullet."

The reporter turned toward the camera. "Okay, we're about to get Flattsville's take on things—wherever that is."

The hillbilly father leaned into the microphone and said, "I done told ya already—it's a stone's throw from Gullet."

Jessica forced another smile. "Do you have an opinion on Jonathan Knight allegedly marrying his stepsister?"

"If *allegedly* means legally, that boy's got every right on earth to marry any gal he's sweet on. After hearin' all the commotion over his choice of a wife, I told the misses here that we gotta get over there and defend Johnson."

"You mean Jonathan."

"Whatever—he needs a spokesman. And that's me. I'm here to speak for our kind."

Jonathan froze as he viewed the live televised interview. "Oh, God. No. No!"

I was speechless and squeezed Jonathan's arm without taking my eyes off the screen.

In a state of shock, Jonathan rose from the sofa and, one guarded step at a time, crossed the room until he planted himself in front of the TV screen. I've never seen anyone have an out-of-body experience before. This was my first.

The hillbilly father continued to speak. "Ya see, a feller can't help who he's smitten with. Sometimes, in the middle of a family gatherin', ya look around, and low and behold, there she is—the one that melts yer heart." He winked at his red-headed wife.

A group of reporters scrambled over to the hillbilly and shoved their mics in front of his face.

The hillbilly father paused a moment to organize his thoughts. Then he spoke again. "I always say love ain't a brain thing." He pointed at the side of his head. Then at his chest. "It's a heart thing. A feller's got no choice in the matter."

Jonathan closed his eyes. "Please, make him stop."

Another reporter asked, "So, you think it's not a problem if siblings marry?"

I shook my fist at the TV screen. "We're not siblings!"

The hillbilly father glanced over his shoulder as if something was gnawing at him in the distance. "I didn't mean to spend this much time talkin' about somethin' that amounts to a pile of nuthin'. I got a stew simmerin' on the campfire that needs tendin' to." As he turned to walk away, he motioned to his wife and kids to follow.

Jonathan breathed a sigh of relief at the sight of the hillbilly walking away.

As I reached for the remote, I muttered, "Thank God. He left."

Jonathan held his hand up. "Leave it on. I need to keep up with what's happening, no matter how painful it is to watch."

The Hillbilly father turned back to the reporters and said, "So if y'all wanna follow me over to my campsite, I'd sure 'nuff be glad to particularize some more."

As the hillbilly family walked away, the TV reporter turned to face her cameraman and said, "And that will do it for now. This is Jessica Picante reporting live from the beach at Santa Barbara."

Jessica Picante touched the IFB in her ear and nodded at whatever instructions she received. As she plodded through the sand in the direction of the hillbilly family, she turned back toward the camera and said, "We've decided to stay right here and keep you all up to date on this story."

Jonathan's voice was lifeless as he said, "This can't be happening."

The herd of reporters followed the hillbillies to the beach campsite.

Picante continued speaking to her viewing audience. "Let's probe a little deeper into this man who claims to be Jonathan Knight's spokesperson."

My mother opened the sliding glass door and glanced at the TV. She asked Jonathan, "How did he get to be your spokesperson?"

"He's *not* my spokesman," Jonathan said. "He's some incestual nut that crawled out of a swamp somewhere to destroy my career."

"Do you think Hyde is paying him?" I asked.

"No. I think he's the real deal. He thinks he's helping us." Jonathan fell back onto the sofa and pressed his palm against his forehead. He continued watching the TV screen while taking quick, shallow breaths.

The makeshift campsite was on the sand, several hundred feet from the wedding site and a few steps from the waves.

The hillbilly father sat on a rugged piece of driftwood next to his youngest son. His wife kneeled beside a large cast-iron pot that rested on a grate above a crackling fire. She used a long-handled ladle to churn the bubbling concoction.

As the reporters crowded around the campsite, one asked, "Does your son have any thoughts about relatives marrying each other?"

"This here youngin'? He can't talk. Never could," said the hillbilly father.

"How about your wife? What does she have to say?" another reporter asked.

"We agreed early on that I was to do the thinkin'. So, to answer yer question, she thinks what *I* think." He handed her a bowl. "Darlin', fetch me up a big ol' helpin' of that gumbo." He smiled and licked his lips at the steaming greenish-brown sludge. "And dig down deep—where the good stuff hides."

It horrified me that this self-appointed hillbilly spokesman proceeded to ruin our lives. With every hillbilly syllable that flowed from his mouth, my lifelong dream of being married slipped farther away, and Jonathan's political aspirations disappeared like a long-handled ladle into a pot of bubbling sludge.

A knock on the hotel door brought me back to the moment.

"It's me! Howie!"

I opened the door, and Howie, Cassie, and Sherman entered. Howie gripped a large envelope in his hand.

Howie said, "Sherman was in the hotel café. I had to get him away from Uncle Arnold's life insurance pitch."

My mother hurried toward Sherman. "There he is! Sweet little Shermy."

Her aggressive bear hug pinned his arms to his sides.

"Don't kill him," I said.

"I just love this boy," my mother said.

"Piper, we decided we're going to put the wedding site back together," Cassie said. "We will not let anyone ruin your dream. We want you to get married tomorrow as planned and on schedule. The weather's good, and we'll restore that damn site if it's the last thing we do."

I became overwhelmed with emotion and hugged Cassie. My eyes filled with tears, and my throat tightened, choking off my ability to speak.

Cassie continued. "And Sherman agreed to pitch in. He'll rebuild the wedding arch. If we have to, we'll use the groomsmen as guards around the site. You're going to have your wedding."

"Oh, hell. Make life easy," my mother said to me. "Just shack up."

I ignored her and hugged Howie and Sherman.

My mother turned to Sherman. "Come sit with us on the balcony, Shermy. It's too stuffy in here—if you know what I mean. You can get to know Walter better."

She grabbed Sherman's arm and pulled him toward the balcony, the way a lion drags its prey.

Howie approached Jonathan. "Who's that on the TV?"

"It's my new spokesman," Jonathan said sarcastically.

Howie and Cassie stared at the TV screen and the hillbilly father.

Cassie turned to Jonathan. "What part of the country are you trying to appeal to?"

"He's not my spokesperson. He gave himself that title. And the reporters are all too willing to go along with it."

Another reporter aimed his microphone at the hillbilly father and asked, "Although it's legal, Americans still consider marriage between step-siblings taboo. But you don't see it that way?"

"Ah, heck no." He rubbed his stubbly chin while contemplating his next profound remark. "Simplify. That's the word of the day, boys. With a step-sibling, there's no need to change yer last name. Life's simpler. Slip a cigar band on her finger, and yer good to go."

Jonathan's face turned pale, and he wasn't moving.

"Breathe," I said.

He took short, shallow breaths and placed his hand on his stomach.

"Jonathan, we can't let this go on a minute longer. You're going to have to make a public statement." I pointed to the TV. "We can't let that nut speak for us. He's ruining everything."

"I got this," Howie said. He moved to the far side of the hotel room and stood in front of the white wall. He opened a large envelope and pulled out a photo of Jonathan and me. Using a push pin, he stuck the image in the center of the wall.

"Why don't you just *tell us* your idea," I said.

Howie picked up the envelope again. "No, this method is much cooler."

As Howie began his demonstration, my mother opened the sliding glass door and headed toward the kitchenette.

Howie looped red yarn around the push pin and stretched it to the left. He pulled a photo of a woman out of the envelope and pinned it to the wall, wrapping the end of the red yarn around its push pin. Howie raised a confident eyebrow. "And there you go."

Jonathan cocked his head to one side. "Who is that?"

"That, my friends, is our next move. Jessica Picante."

I nudged Jonathan. "She's the reporter on the beach."

Jonathan rubbed both temples with his fingers. "Really, Howie? You could've made your point with one sentence. I'm trying to eliminate drama. This," he pointed at the wall, "adds to it."

Cassie held a finger in the air. "He may be on to something."

Howie's eyes widened at the sound of Cassie's supportive

voice.

I exhaled. "Oh, good, Cass. I'm glad you could see where he was going. For a minute there, I thought Howie was planning to kidnap Jessica Picante."

Cassie laughed. "Sorry, Howie. I didn't mean to interrupt your plan. Go on."

Howie's eyes darted back and forth. "Uh… I, uh… Cassie, where did *you* think I was headed with this?"

My voice filled with alarm. "So, you *were* thinking of kidnapping Jessica Picante."

Howie shook his head at the suggestion. "Of course not. That's crazy talk. Go ahead, Cassie. You knew what I was thinking. Right?"

"Not really."

"Guess. C'mon. Just for fun." Howie gestured with his hand for her to continue.

Cassie's eyes pointed at the floor. "Well, maybe, just maybe, setting up an interview might be a good idea. You know, like we all talked about before. It's a way to let people hear your story in your own words, without any filter. You can explain the innocent way this all came about."

Howie's smile grew with every word Cassie said. "I like it."

I said to Howie. "That wasn't your plan. Admit it."

Howie kicked at the floor with his shoe. "Yeah. It was. Sure."

I turned to Jonathan. "Honey, what do you think? Should we do this?"

"I don't think we have much choice."

My mother glided back across the room with a third wine glass. The sight on the TV screen stopped her in her tracks. "Look at this."

The others gathered in front of the TV. On the screen, a group of protesters held signs disparaging Jonathan's character and marched to the steady cadence of a drum.

Jessica Picante approached the angry woman with the drum and held a microphone to her mouth. "Care to make a comment about Jonathan Knight?"

Jonathan and I leaned closer to the screen and, at the same time, muttered, "Tonya?"

My mother giggled. "It *is* her!"

As Tanya beat a drum with one hand, she leaned close to the microphone. "Screw Jonathan Knight, that effing bastard!"

My mother shook her head and smiled. "Typical Tonya. Always full of surprises. I didn't know she could play a musical instrument."

Jonathan glared at my mother. "Thanks for getting Tanya involved in our wedding. That was helpful."

Walter hurried in to find out what the commotion was all about.

The TV screen flashed the words *Breaking News!*

A news anchor sitting at a newsroom desk shuffled a few papers and cleared his throat. "This just in. Researchers have just released the latest poll numbers from a telephone survey concerning the race for the twenty-fourth Congressional district. This won't be good news for challenger Jonathan Knight. He had been closing in on the incumbent, Malcolm Hyde, until news broke that he is currently involved in a romantic relationship with his stepsister."

I screamed at the TV. "We're not blood relatives!"

It was my turn to glare at my mother.

Jonathan glared at Walter.

Howie said, "They make it sound a lot weirder than it is."

"A lot weirder than it is?" I asked. "So you also think we're weird?"

The news anchor continued. "Among likely voters, Knight's approval ratings have dropped into the single digits. Unless Knight figures out some way to undo the damage and turn things around, Hyde can look forward to serving his eleventh term in office. Let's go live back to the beach and see if Jessica Picante has a reaction to the latest polls from Jonathan Knight's new spokesperson…"

"Howie," Jonathan said, "Set up the interview with Jessica Picante."

CHAPTER 21

Jonathan, Howie, Cassie, and I climbed into Howie's car and traveled the thirty-five-mile trip south to the satellite studio of L.A.'s Action News Six. It was twilight, and the streets of the small city of Oxnard were as lovely as the name itself.

Howie had volunteered to drive so that Jonathan and I might clear our minds and prepare for the prime-time interview with Jessica Picante. Howie's time as the driver didn't last long; a whole twelve minutes. After running a stop sign, nearly missing a jogger, and making three wrong turns, Cassie took over the driving duties.

Jonathan remained subdued and contemplative for most of the trip.

"There it is!" Cassie said. "The Channel Six studio."

I placed my hand over Jonathan's and squeezed it, reassuring him.

A lighted sign with a white number six on a blue background illuminated the sidewalk in front of a one-story studio. Action News Six was sandwiched between two local businesses. On one side was an eatery claiming to be Oxnard's second-best barbeque. On the other side was a salon named Janet Nail. Obviously, the folks at Janet Nail specialized in manicures, not grammar.

We waited at the studio's front door until Jessica Picante herself opened it. She flashed a toothy smile and ushered us into the studio. She greeted Howie first with an enormous hug.

"I'm Jonathan's campaign manager," Howie said.

Jessica tilted her head to one side, and her lips turned to a pout. "You must be overwhelmed with all that's going on. Bless your heart."

She moved on to Cassie. "And you are?"

"I'm Cassie. Piper's maid of honor. I'm here to support her."

"How fortunate is she to have a friend like you? To stick by her when most wouldn't. You are just adorable. Talk later?"

Cassie nodded.

Next, Jessica hugged me. "And you must be Piper. I can't tell you how much my heart goes out to you—poor thing. A bride-to-be has enough to worry about as it is. Being caught in the middle of political dirty tricks right before your wedding is an unthinkable act of cruelty no woman deserves."

While Jessica was giving me an extra-long hug, I glanced at Jonathan and mouthed the words, *she's so nice!*

Jessica pulled back, but held both of my hands in hers. "I feel an instant connection with you, Piper. When this is all over, I think we could be great friends. Unfortunately for me, I'm meeting you too late to be your maid of honor."

I blushed.

Cassie feigned a smile.

Jessica let go of my hands and picked up Jonathan's. She said, "Mr. Knight. What a pleasure it is to meet you, sir."

"Just call me Jonathan."

"And isn't that just like you?" Jessica said. "Humble to a fault."

"Well, I—"

"What you are dealing with is unbelievable. I've known Hyde for a long time. He's capable of anything when he feels threatened, and I'm sure he's the force behind everything you're going through."

"I'm glad you recognize that." Jonathan fake-wiped his forehead with a quick sweep of his hand. "Whew!"

Jessica locked onto Jonathan's eyes. "I want you to know how appreciative I am that you chose me for this big interview. I consider it an honor."

"I'd like to take all the credit for that, but Howie chose you, thinking you'd be the fairest to us."

She turned toward Howie. "How sweet is that? Thank you for your confidence. Jonathan's lucky to have you by his side." To Jonathan, she said, "*Fair* is my middle name." She winked.

Jessica pointed to three blue upholstered chairs placed around a small coffee table. "Piper, Jonathan, you both have a seat there. I'll be with you in a minute. Oh, and by the way, Cassie, I love your shoes. You'll have to share with me later where you shop." She motioned for Cassie and Howie to follow her. She led them to a small sofa along the back wall behind three TV cameras.

A sound technician approached Jonathan and me. He clipped a lapel mic on each of us and hid small transmitter packs behind us on our clothing.

Jonathan and I sat in two chairs placed close together. A large flat TV screen covered the entire wall behind us.

A man with a bag full of makeup and brushes attached to a long shoulder strap hurried toward us. He dabbed at each of our faces with a powdery makeup brush.

Out of the corner of Jonathan's mouth, he said to me, "This should be good. I think she's sympathetic and on our side. And very professional."

The makeup artist scoffed at that description. In a whispered voice, he said, "She was a greeter at Walmart before this job. She married the station owner."

"Still, she has to have talent to perform at this level," Jonathan replied.

The makeup artist finished and left without saying another word.

"I'm so nervous," I said. "I'm not used to this."

"I understand, but just be yourself. We're lucky to have Jessica Picante interviewing us. She'll be fair."

"I feel like we didn't talk enough about what to say. I don't want to make a mistake and say something stupid."

Jonathan said, "And that's exactly why Howie's not part of this interview."

"I heard that," Howie's voice uttered from the darkened part of the studio.

Jonathan continued. "All we need to do is tell the truth. We don't need to prepare for that. We'll simply explain that we were engaged long before we learned your mom and my dad once knew each other. And their last-minute marriage has nothing to do with *our* relationship."

"I'm still nervous."

Jessica returned to the main studio and sat across from us in the third blue chair. She smiled and thanked us again for the interview.

A woman in her twenties wearing a headset approached them and said, "Stand by." She stepped back and stood next to the middle camera. She held up her hand and counted down from the number four, using her fingers. After three fingers were counted, she pointed at Jessica.

Jessica faced the middle camera. "I'm Jessica Picante. Welcome to Action News Six's Movers and Shakers, a nightly news segment featuring the day's hot topics and the people behind them. Tonight's live interview features Congressional candidate Jonathan Knight who has found himself in a bit of controversy of late."

Jessica swiveled her chair toward Jonathan. "Welcome."

"Thank you for having us," he said.

Jessica's smile disappeared, and her eyes narrowed. "Running for Congress is a huge undertaking, and this is the first time you've run for office. Is that correct?"

"That's right."

"So, the first office you decide to run for is a seat in the US Congress?"

"Right."

Jessica paused a moment and rested her hand on her chin. "You weren't in the State Senate?"

"No."

"Were you a county supervisor?"

"No."

"Surely, you were a city councilman."

"You were correct when you said it was my first campaign."

Jessica used a subtle shake of her head to convey her opinion to the viewing audience. "At least you served on a school board at some time in your past. Right?"

Jonathan glanced at me. I'm sure my mouth was open.

Jonathan said, "I'm not really a politician. I just wanted to make a difference."

"Did you ever"—Jessica's fingers made air quotes—"*make a difference* on the board of a PTA?"

"No. I don't have kids."

"Oh. Is having a child a requirement to serve on a PTA board?"

"Uh, maybe not."

"Let's move on," Jessica said. "It was discovered that you asked your step-sister to marry you. Is that right?"

Jonathan's face became flushed, and beads of perspiration oozed down his forehead. "Well, uh—"

"It's not a hard question."

Jonathan squirmed in his seat. "It's complicated. You see—"

Jessica nodded her head toward me. "Well, is she your stepsister, or isn't she?"

I squinted to the area behind the cameras and spotted Howie's hands covering his face.

Jessica turned to the middle camera. "Jonathan Knight's stepsister is also with us tonight."

I cleared my tight throat before speaking. "I'd like to explain that—"

"I'm sorry to cut you off, but I'll get to you in a minute."

My heart raced, and adrenaline pumped through my every limb. To most observers, I probably appeared to be calm, but my muscles twitched, and I couldn't stop jiggling my heels. Something had taken over my body like I'd never before experienced. It was as if I had the strength that is sometimes exhibited when a pedestrian lifts a car off a trapped person. If necessary, I was prepared to lift the entire studio that just ran over Jonathan. But a lot was on the line, and I wasn't sure what to do, so I sat quietly and waited for Jonathan to gain control of the situation.

Jessica continued questioning Jonathan. "I guess it wouldn't be so scandalous that you're marrying your stepsister if you hadn't campaigned as the candidate who's returning things back to"—she used her air quotes again—"*normal*."

"I—"

She cut Jonathan off again and continued her speech. "But hypocrisy is alive and well these days. It appears that you believe your relationship is not only acceptable, but your campaign actually promotes this behavior."

"What? I never promoted or endorsed anything of the kind."

"That's not what your spokesman says." She turned her head to the huge monitor on the wall. "Watch this video clip."

The hillbilly father's face took up most of the screen. His twang pierced the air. "…he needs a spokesman. And that's me. I'm here to speak for our kind." A video cut, then, "…the minute I laid eyes on this feller, Jonathan, I said to the missus here, if he ain't one of us, I don't know who is. He's my kind of people." Another video cut. "Sometimes, in the middle of a family gathering, ya look around, and low and behold, there she is." Another rough video cut. "I always say, love ain't a brain thing, it's a heart thing. I speak for him and everyone else back in Flattsville."

"Jonathan, are you from Flattsville, too?"

"No."

"You are aware that you must be a resident of the district in order to represent it, right?"

"I was born here, in Santa Barbara. I don't even know where Flattsville is."

Howie tried to help Jonathan. He cupped his hands and said, "It's a stone's throw from Gullet."

Jessica's face revealed she wasn't amused, and she glared at Jonathan. "He sounds like a spokesman to me."

"He is not my spokesman."

"Oh, I think he is."

"I have no clue who the guy is."

Jessica shook her head at Jonathan. "Before now, have you made any attempt to disavow his role in your campaign publicly?"

"Uh, no, but I—"

"If he has no connection to your campaign, do you think you should have made at least a minimal effort to refute the opinions of your spokesman?"

Jonathan fixed his eyes on the floor. "Maybe I should have."

"Congressman Hyde insists that's your official spokesperson."

"I assure you he's not—"

Jessica swiveled her chair toward me. "As his stepsister—"

I jumped out of my chair and hovered over Jessica.

"Piper, please," Jonathan said as he grabbed my arm and tried to pull me back.

I jerked my arm free and put my face inches from Jessica's. "You want answers? I'll give you answers!"

Jessica's eyes filled with terror. As she leaned back and away from me, she said, "I'm in control—"

"Be quiet. You say you want answers, but you don't. You interrupt every time we talk."

Cassie shouted through cupped hands near her mouth, "Whoo-hoo! You go, girl!" I glanced over as she jutted her fist in the air.

Howie peeked through his fingers.

I turned back to Jessica. "I'm going to explain the circumstance we've found ourselves in—not to you, but to your audience—and you are not going to butt in and twist everything!"

"But—"

"Do you not listen? I said be quiet!"

Jessica raised both eyebrows, and her bottom lip quivered. She held her palms up in surrender mode.

"Now, in a nutshell—Jonathan and I met months ago. I fell in love with him at first sight. He's a good man. And just to be crystal clear, we were not related in any way. Days from marrying, we introduced my single mother to his widowed dad. One thing led to another, and they married on a whim —yesterday! Not years ago. Yesterday! I couldn't stop them if I tried. What happened between my mother and his father technically created some artificial connection between Jonathan and me. Despite that, we're no different from any other couple. No crazy hillbilly or sleazy greaseball member of Congress like Malcolm Hyde can make me feel like I'm doing anything wrong by marrying Jonathan. Because I'm not! And just so you're clear on this—we're getting married tomorrow! On the same damn beach where we planned to marry before the storm. And you're not invited! Now! Any more questions?"

Jessica Picante had leaned as far back in her chair as possible. She trembled with fear, and she was speechless. She answered by shaking her head.

"Good." I stood up straight, ripped off and tossed away my lapel mic, and put my arm through Jonathan's. "If you happen to think of any more idiotic, misleading, manipulative questions, we'll be next door enjoying Oxnard's Second-best Barbeque. And I'm told they're hiring a greeter for their front door. When you're booted from here for lack of talent, try that next. And consider it a step up."

Jessica Picante turned toward the camera and signaled for the crew to cut to the Burbank studio by swiping her finger across her throat.

The Burbank studio anchor appeared on the big screen and said, "We might have just witnessed the end of the short political career of Jonathan Knight."

CHAPTER 22

The atmosphere in the car made the thirty-five-mile journey back to Santa Barbara feel like one thousand and thirty-five miles. The mood was somber. A time for a serious reassessment of our failed strategy. Cassie drove north on Highway 101 while Howie sat in the front passenger seat playing Candy Crush on his phone. Oncoming headlights illuminated their faces with sporadic flashes of light. Jonathan and I were in the backseat, my face pressed against his chest, covering his once clean and pressed dress shirt with tears and eyeliner.

Over the last few days, I became so accustomed to feeling sick to my stomach that I rode this current wave of nausea like an expert surfer. Well, that's what I'd like to believe. Truth is, I rolled down the window, hung my head out of the car, and lost seven bucks worth of barbecued pork. I finished and wiped my mouth on Jonathan's sleeve. My wind-blown hair covered my pitiful face, and that was fine with me.

Between sobs, I muttered. "I'm so sorry. I ruined your chances of being elected."

Jonathan didn't respond.

"Are you mad at me?" I asked.

He exhaled and stared out the window at the darkness.

"Would you please say something?"

Without looking at me, he said, "You could've let me handle it. I looked weak."

"You didn't look weak. You were just weighing all the ramifications of speaking up. That's what smart people do. I'm the one who let emotions get the best of me."

"I've been so cautious. So careful. I won't even pass by a window without thinking twice."

I put my hand on his. "You've been very disciplined."

Still gazing out the window, Jonathan said, "I wanted to lash out at Jessica Picante. I did. But I also wanted to serve a term in congress. And not for any other reason than to make a difference. I wanted it so bad, but I was too cautious. I realized the error of my inaction the moment you jumped all over her. I was the one who should've shown courage. It was bad enough that I sat passively and let her jerk me around. Now, my fiancé looks more like a leader. I lose either way. You were the strong one tonight. I'm the one who blew it."

"If I'm that strong, why am I crying?" I lifted my face off Jonathan's chest to see Cassie's eyes in the rearview mirror. "How bad did I blow it, Cass? You're always honest with me."

Cassie glanced in the rearview mirror at me. "I don't know about the politics of it all. I *do* know that you were awesome. You kicked ass. And to answer your question, yes, Jonathan probably couldn't be elected dogcatcher right now."

"I don't think they elect dogcatchers," Howie said. Then he lowered his voice, whispering to Cassie. "Jonathan wouldn't be interested in that, anyway."

"It's an expression," Cassie said.

I leaned back and closed my eyes. "I just feel sick."

Howie said, "That's Oxnard's Second-best Barbeque. I feel it too."

"Piper, you stood up for the man you love. No one can blame you for that," Cassie said.

I stared into the night, and my mind replayed my studio outburst over and over.

Howie turned toward the backseat. "Jonathan, how are you doing?"

Jonathan gazed out the window at the moon sinking over the

ocean.

Howie tried again. "Jonathan?"

"I'll be alright. But I do want to say that I'm proud of Piper. What she did is one reason I love her so much. But politics is a tough game. I'm at the mercy of the media and public opinion. I guess I wasn't meant to be a member of Congress."

His words caused me to shed another river of tears.

As we traveled, the silence became awkward.

"Howie, turn on the radio for some noise," Cassie said.

Howie turned the knob and stopped at a voice that mentioned the Oxnard TV interview.

Cassie shook her head at him. "They don't want to hear that."

Howie turned up the volume, and the announcer's voice broke the silence. "This is not surprising. Flash polls show Jonathan Knight has closed the gap in his race with Congressman Hyde. In fact, he's slightly ahead."

I sat up.

Howie cheered, and Cassie pumped her fist in the air.

The radio show's host continued. "Our phone board here at the station has been lit up like a Christmas tree ever since the interview. They all agree that Jessica Picante deserved that scolding."

"No way!" I said.

"The viewers loved it," the radio show's host said. "Our callers are saying the fighting spirit they witnessed tonight is just the thing we need in Washington, DC. And I couldn't agree more."

Tears continued to stream down my cheeks, but now they were tears of joy. I wanted to kiss Jonathan on the lips, but he pulled back the way a normal person pulls back when they're about to be kissed by someone who just threw up. Anyway, what appeared to be a total disaster minutes ago had turned into a surprising victory.

Jonathan's lips formed a half smile. "I learned a lesson tonight," he said. "Next time I'll stand up for what I know is the truth. I won't be pushed around anymore. And if I need help, I can sic Piper on them."

"Oh, so I'm your dog?" I said, adding a flirty tone.

"I'm joking. Hey, I better be quiet. I don't want to end up on the wrong end of one of your famous rants."

We all chuckled.

"Remember, the interview was my idea," Howie said. "But I can't take all the credit."

I arrived at the door of my hotel room. Jonathan was right behind me. As I slid the key card through the scanner, I said, "It's the night before our wedding. You're not supposed to be in my room. It's tradition."

"Just let me come in for a minute. We need to celebrate a little."

I flipped on the light and let out a short scream. "Mother!"

My mother sat in a chair, staring at nothing in particular.

"Mother?"

She didn't respond.

"Mother? Hello?"

Still no response.

I walked over to her and nudged her on the shoulder. "Are you alright?"

She snapped out of her trance-like state. Her eyes lifted to find me.

"Oh. Piper."

"Why were you sitting in the dark? What's going on?"

"Yes, I am," she muttered.

"Mother, I didn't ask *if* you were sitting in the dark. I'm asking *why*?"

"Thinking."

"Something's wrong. Did you and Walter have an argument?"

"Huh? What?"

"I asked if you and Walter had a fight."

She didn't respond right away. After several seconds, she answered, "Oh, no. We're fine."

"Then what's wrong?"

She forced a laugh and waved off any concern. "It's nothing. Sometimes I let my imagination get the best of me."

I turned to Jonathan. "Sweetie, would you give us a minute?"

Jonathan asked, "Is she okay?"

"I think so. Give us a few minutes."

"No problem. I'll be in my room. Call me when you're done, so I can say goodnight."

As Jonathan headed back to his hotel room, I turned to my mother. "Okay. Talk to me. What's up?"

She stood and paced the floor. "I'm just being silly. It's nothing. Really."

"Then why are you pacing? Are you having second thoughts about marrying Walter? If you are, sometimes people go through that. It's all new to you. Give it some time."

"No, no. It's not that."

"Then what is it?"

"Okay. I'll tell you, but you're going to laugh."

I sat across from her on the sofa and folded my arms. "Fine. Make me laugh."

Her eyes scanned the room. "Do you have any wine? Or something stronger?"

I took a deep breath. "Mother, it's getting late. Stop stalling. I'm getting married tomorrow and don't want bags under my eyes."

She swallowed. "Well, Wally and I were talking, and I asked him if he'd do something for me."

"Go on."

"I asked him to keep an open mind about it."

"Mother. Get to the point, please."

"I told him that you would be walking barefoot on the sand tomorrow, and I asked Walter if he'd join me in being barefoot, too."

I laughed. "Mother, I appreciate it, but it doesn't matter."

"Well, he said no. There's no way he would be barefoot. Piper, I really wanted to support you in that way."

"So that's what this was all about? Being barefoot at my

wedding? Mother, you scared me. I thought something was really wrong."

"There's more. So then I kept insisting that he be barefoot, and he got annoyed. When he gets cranky, he has these little wrinkles between his eyebrows. Two vertical lines—like an eleven."

"Where's this story going?"

"Piper, are you sure there's no wine here?"

"Don't worry about the wine. Just get to the point."

She took a deep breath. "So, I happen to mention that he and Jonathan have that same little set of wrinkles between their eyebrows. Funny right?

"Not yet."

"Are you absolutely sure there's not any wine left?"

My silent stare was my response.

"Well, that's a bummer," she said.

"Would you continue, please?"

"Okay, Okay. Where was I? Oh, right. Anyway, when I mentioned that they looked alike, Wally told me that was impossible. So, I asked why. And he said it was because Jonathan was adopted."

I breathed a sigh of relief. "That's it? I already knew that. There's nothing to worry about. Adoption is a beautiful thing."

"Oh, right. Totally."

"Walter said the girl he met right after me—Jonathan's mother—told him upfront that she couldn't have children. So, when they married, Walter's father pulled a few strings, and they adopted a boy right away. They were still in New York."

"Okay, but why are you thinking about this the night before my wedding?" I studied my mother's face. "You're still nervous. Is there something else?"

She cocked her head a bit as if she were trying to remember.

I wasn't buying her act. "There's something else. I can tell."

My mother forced a smile. "There is a little more to the story, and this is the part where you're going to think I'm crazy."

"I don't need a little more to the story to arrive at that

conclusion."

"Well, around the time that Wally and I split, I began dating several boys at once. Make love, not war, right?"

"You were on the rebound. It's okay. It happens."

"So, as fate would have it, I found myself a little preggo, if you know what I mean. Piper, I wanted to have that baby and raise it, but I was in no financial position to do that. Do you understand?"

I got up from the sofa and hugged her. "If you have regrets, I understand."

"Piper, I *had* that baby. I never told you this."

I pulled back to see her face. After a moment, I stood and began to search every cupboard and drawer in the suite.

"What are you doing?" she asked.

I continued to scour the room. "Where is that damn wine when we need it?"

She grabbed me by the shoulders. "Piper. Stop."

"Sorry. I just wasn't expecting this." I took a moment to compose myself. "Did that baby find you? She did, didn't she? Oh, my God, she contacted you!"

"Piper, it was a baby boy."

"So, *he* contacted you?"

"Not exactly."

We both sat down on the edge of the sofa.

I tried to shake off my confusion. "Mother, please. Get to the point."

"I'm trying. Anyway, I gave that baby up for adoption right after the birth. I didn't want to meet the adoptive parents because it was all just too hard on me."

"Okay. I understand. Did you tell the father about this?"

Her eyes pointed away. "I'm a little embarrassed to admit that I couldn't figure out which guy was the father. I lost track of everyone I dated and had no way of tracking them down. New York City is a big place. And this is where my imagination gets a little carried away. This is the funny part." She swallowed again. "I had that baby around Christmastime."

"That's the time of year Jonathan was born—" my heart pounded, and I stood. "Oh, God. When did you and Walter break up?"

My mother cringed. "Earlier that year. In the spring."

I paced the floor with urgency and held my hand to my head. "Mother, what day was that baby born?"

"I was sedated and out of it. I can't remember the date exactly. I purposely didn't want to remember that baby's birthdate for emotional reasons."

I continued to pace, but now with both hands holding my head. "Are you saying that there's a chance that Jonathan is my... my..."

"Brother?" she helped me finish my sentence.

"I think I'm going to throw up! Again."

She stood and wrapped her arm around me. I removed her arms and continued pacing.

She said, "Now see? I got you all freaked out. Let's both calm down. Really, sweetie, there's no chance Jonathan is that baby. Even if he *was* born in that hospital on that very day, several babies were given up for adoption when I was there. So even if Jonathan was born on whatever day and in the same hospital, that still wouldn't prove he's mine. A one out of three chance at best."

I threw my hands up. "Oh, that's comforting. Only a thirty-three percent chance I'm marrying my brother." I raised my voice. "Who would worry about that?"

"Stay calm, sweetie. You two don't even look alike."

I stopped in my tracks. "Our middle fingers! They're the same. We joked about it!"

"Huh?"

"Our middle fingers—they're longer than the others." I held up my middle finger in front of her face. "See?"

"Everybody's middle finger is the longest. I should know. I've seen plenty of them."

"Mother, several times over the last few days you've commented on how much Jonathan and I look alike!"

"I didn't really mean it. That was just chit-chat."

I had a hard time catching my breath. My brain spun in circles.

"Are you having a panic attack?" she asked.

"Yes! And I'm entitled! The night before my wedding, I find out there's a chance my fiancé is my... my..."

"Brother?"

"Mother! Stop finishing my sentences! Especially with that... that B-word!" I kept pacing. "Wait. I need to relax. There's no way Jonathan is that baby you gave away. I would know if he were my..." I wagged my finger at her. "Don't say it! Anyway, a woman knows this kind of thing. My senses would tell me. If it were true, kissing him would feel repulsive. That's how nature works."

"Sweetie, I've ruined your life."

I was defiant and shook my head. "No, you didn't, because Jonathan is not your son. You'd know if he were. Like me, you'd sense it."

She drew in a long breath. "At the restaurant, I did say that you and Jonathan were beginning to look alike!"

"Again, not helping. Wait! Those other guys you dated—what did they look like? That might ease my mind."

"They all looked like Wally. That's why I dated them."

I collapsed on the sofa and sobbed. "I have to call off the wedding."

"Why?"

"Why? You're asking me why? I'll tell you why. Because if he turns out to be my... my... you know what—not only would it be revolting and disgusting, but it would also be against the law."

She patted my back as I lay on my side, crying.

She said, "Please don't cry. Everything will be totally cool. You'll see. This will be our little secret."

"Mother! No way! Until I confirm everything's fine, I'm calling off the wedding!"

"I'm willing to keep it a secret. No one will ever know."

I raised my head off the sofa. "If it turns out to be true, I'll know. Jonathan will know. Everyone will know!"

"How?"

"I don't want to say."

"Sweetie, how will they know?"

I clenched my teeth. Then I said, "If we have a kid, he'll eventually go to school. In music class, when the other kids are choosing drums, harps, trumpets—our kid will be drawn to the… the…" I fell back onto the sofa, and between sobs, I groaned, "…the banjo!"

My mother stood and placed one hand on her hip and nodded. "I knew there was a problem when I read Jonathan's palm."

"I don't believe in palm reading," I said, closing my eyes for a split second before they popped open again. "Ok, what'd you see?" I sat up.

"It wasn't good. His marriage line terminated at the family line, and they both converged at the middle finger. But don't go by that, sweetie. I'm a little rusty at it. I haven't been accurate since Uncle Joe died."

I choked back tears long enough to ask, "You read his palm? Really? What did you see?"

"Blood." She crinkled her nose. "I told him he'd live. But a tree had just fallen on him."

I covered my face with my hands and cried. "This is the worst day of my life. Tomorrow was supposed to be the best day of my life."

She handed me a box of tissues.

Someone knocked on the door.

"Don't answer it," I said. "I can't face anyone right now."

My mother ignored me and tip-toed to the door. "Who is it?"

"Jonathan."

Her eyes widened, and she turned to me for help.

Horrified, I peeked over the tissue I held at my nose. I wiped my eyes and whispered, "I can't tell him anything right now. I just can't."

She opened the door and let Jonathan into the suite.

He approached me and asked, "Have you been crying?"

I didn't respond. Instead, I tried to stop my body from shaking.

"Aw, the emotions of a bride," he said.

My bottom lip quivered.

He sat down on the sofa and leaned in to kiss me. "Your beautiful, even when you're crying."

I leaned away. "What are you doing?"

"Kissing you goodnight."

I shook my head. "We can't. It goes against tradition. In fact, you shouldn't be here at all the night before the wedding."

"Doesn't that superstition only apply to the day of the wedding?"

"In some families. In mine, it's the night before too."

"Your family's tradition? But no one has married for generations."

"Because they kissed the night before. See? Bad luck."

He smiled and leaned forward again. "Goodnight," he said as he puckered his lips.

I leaned away and turned my head.

He laughed. "Oh, c'mon. We've kissed a thousand times."

"Let's not think about that."

He smiled, puckered again, and leaned forward.

I pulled back more. "I'm not bucking tradition. I told you, kissing the night before flies right in the face of tradition."

Jonathan's brow furrowed. "We're about to be married by a guy from the Church of Planetary Unification. I didn't think you were *that* into tradition."

I diverted my eyes from him. "Goodnight, Jonathan."

Jonathan's shoulders slumped as he opened the door to leave. He was about to close the door behind him when he stopped and turned back toward me. "I miss kissing you goodnight. But it's okay. Tomorrow night, we'll be sleeping together."

"We'll see," I said.

Jonathan tilted his head to one side as my mother closed the door on him.

CHAPTER 23

With Jonathan out of my hotel room, I leaped off the sofa. I grabbed my mother's shoulders with both hands. "Mother, what do I do? This ruins everything!"

"I wish there was some way I could prove the baby I gave away was not Jonathan, but I just don't know how."

I pulled my mobile phone from my pocket and dialed. "Cass. I need you"

"Why? I was about to soak in a warm bath."

"There's no time for that. Just come here."

"Not another crisis. I thought everything was fine now."

"It's not. I'll explain when you get here." I hung up.

Nausea hit me like a freight train, and I scurried to the bathroom.

Seconds later, a thud told me the hotel door had shut, and I assumed it was Cassie.

I left the bathroom door open to hear their conversation.

Cassie asked, "Harmony, why is there a look of terror in your eyes?"

"It's bad. It's real bad," my mother said.

I heaved again into the toilet.

Cassie must have heard my dry heave. She asked, "What's *that* all about?"

"It's Piper. Thinking about her future."

"I'll come back another time."

"No. Piper needs you."

When I completed what I hoped was my last heave, I took a swig of mouthwash and walked back into the suite's living room. Cassie was seated in a corner chair.

My mother was still pacing and wringing her hands. She said, "Cassie, you better have a seat."

"I *am* seated."

I was relieved Cassie was there. I needed her. Most maids of honor would've run like hell from me by now. But Cassie thinks Howie's normal, so she can put up with a lot. Still, she braced for the worst.

"What's wrong now?" Cassie asked.

My mind was mush, and I didn't know where to start. I stared at the floor, thinking. "You better have a seat," I said.

"Am I invisible? I *am* seated." Cassie shot my mother a look of concern.

"Oh, right. Right. Of course you are," I said.

While sobbing and pulling tissues from a box, I recounted my mother's story of how it was possible that Jonathan was that baby boy she gave up for adoption thirty years ago.

Cassie sat frozen with her mouth open. This was *not* the type of story to tell anyone who still has a stomach full of Oxnard's Second-best Barbecue. She locked her eyes into a straight-ahead position, and she was non-responsive. My mother nudged her, poked her, and submerged her hand into the icy cold slush of a champagne bucket until she showed some signs of coherence. As she rejoined us, she said, "Uh, Piper, you can't get married tomorrow."

My lower lip quivered. "You're right." I turned to my mother. "She's right."

My mother offered a sliver of hope. "Unless you can prove to yourself by morning that Jonathan is not that baby."

"Mother, I *know* he's not. At least deep down inside, I know it," I said.

Cassie, still staring straight ahead, said, "You're just going to have to ask Walter if he ever met Jonathan's biological mother."

"No!" my mother and I said at the same time.

"That's a no-win situation," my mother added. "Even if he says he *did* meet her, and everything was cool, he'll think we're nuts."

"Irreparably nuts," I added.

"I could have Florina look into her crystal ball," my mother said.

"Mother, this situation calls for reliable and scientific proof. Not a crystal ball!"

"But the ball will show the moment the hospital handed my baby boy to the couple. We'll see if it was Walter!"

"Crystal balls don't see into the past; they see into the future! Wait. What am I saying? Her crystal ball doesn't see *anything*. It came from Party City."

"I got it!" Cassie sprang from her chair, knocking the champagne bucket to the floor. "What the hell is that? And why is my hand numb?" she asked, looking at the bucket.

"That's my mother's doing. Never mind that. What's your idea?"

"Your neighbor—Sherman," Cassie said. "Doesn't he work in a lab? A lab that can run DNA tests?"

"Yes! I love you, Cass!"

I dialed Sherman. "Pick up—Pick up—Pick up—C'mon, Sherman, pick up... Oh, hi! Sherman, it's Piper."

"How are you?" he asked.

"I love that boy," my mother said.

I shushed my mother and resumed my phone conversation. "I'm fine, Sherman. Well, not so fine, really. Sorry to call you this late. I have to ask a favor of you. I realize your lab specializes in criminal cases, but can you run a test for me to see if two people are related?"

"Easy."

I flashed the thumbs-up sign to Cassie and my mother.

My mother placed her hand on her chest to calm her heart. Cassie exhaled.

"I happen to be looking at my own DNA right now," Sherman said.

"You're in the lab right now? At this hour?"

"I didn't mean at this moment. I meant; I've been conducting a DNA test at work. Right now, I'm home, watching Star Wars."

"So, tell me, how would I go about getting a DNA test done?"

"Come in after your honeymoon. I'll get right to it."

"No, that's not going to work. I'll explain later, but it's crucial I get test results by morning."

"By morning? I can't. Luke Skywalker is about to learn who his father is."

"Well, right now it's more important Jonathan learn who his mother is."

"What?"

"Never mind. Just trust me, everything depends on these results."

"Test results by morning? Seriously, Piper?"

"That's right. Morning."

"I'm not sure that's possible. There's a lot of work that goes into doing a DNA test."

"Can you get into the lab tonight?"

"I'm not supposed to be there in the off hours."

"Sherman, can you get into the lab tonight?"

The Star Wars theme was blaring in the background of Sherman's condo until he muted it. "If I have to."

"Yes. You have to."

"The lab keeps a key under the mat."

"Really?"

"For me. I kept showing up to work after forgetting my keys."

I asked, "So, tell me how I can get you samples?"

In great detail, Sherman explained the procedure I needed to follow to get the DNA samples.

My heart filled with hope at the possibility of my worst fears being gone by morning. All I had to do was collect the required DNA samples. This was no task for the faint-hearted. My dreams, hopes, future children, and happiness depended on Sherman—a man who can't walk ten feet without stumbling. And also, on a laboratory whose best idea for security is a key under the mat.

As I ended my call with Sherman, a plan formed in my head.

Well, not really a plan. Not even a partial plan. More accurately, the first step of what might *eventually* be a plan.

I said, "Jonathan has two key cards. We need to get our hands on one of them."

"And why would we need to do that?" Cassie asked.

"We need to get into his room to get a sample from his body. And we need access to that body."

"Body? Sounds like a murder mystery," my mother said.

My nostrils flared as I glared at her. "If the DNA test results don't work out, there'll be a murder alright, but it won't be a mystery."

My mother swallowed hard.

"Mother, hang here for a minute. Cassie, you come with me."

Cassie and I crept down the hotel's hallway. When we reached Jonathan's hotel room door, we paused.

I whispered, "Once we're inside, I'll distract him, and you grab one of the key cards on the dresser. Don't be obvious about it. He can't know what we're doing."

Cassie trembled a bit and acknowledged the instructions with a nod.

A voice boomed from behind us, sounding like a cannon shot. "Hello, ladies," Jonathan said.

CHAPTER 24

We both whirled around.

"Oh, honey, you scared us," I said.

"I ran down to the lobby to get this." He held up a tube of toothpaste.

We stared at the toothpaste.

"Piper?" Jonathan asked.

"What?"

"Can I help you two with anything?"

I'm sure my expression was blank while my brain scrambled for an answer. "Can we go inside?"

Jonathan swiped his key card, and we followed him in.

He turned and faced us. "So, what's up?"

I cleared my throat several times. "Oh. Right. Uh, I just wanted to say that I'm sorry I was short with you when you tried to kiss me goodnight."

"Okay. Fine. And you needed Cassie with you for this?"

Cassie cut in. "I made her do this. As the maid of honor, I wanted to be here to make sure she apologized."

I did a double-take at her. Her ad-lib was unexpected, but quite impressive.

Jonathan put his arms out toward me and puckered his lips.

I straight-armed him while leaning back. "Jonathan, the superstition about kissing the night before the wedding still applies."

"Oh, c'mon!"

"Sorry. It does." I took his arm and pulled him to the other side of the room, away from Cassie. "I didn't want you to go to bed upset—especially if we get married tomorrow."

"*If* we get married?"

"Silly me. I meant to say *when* we get married tomorrow." I placed my hands on his upper arms and turned him so that he faced away from Cassie. My eyes darted back and forth between Jonathan and Cassie.

"Seriously, are you okay?" he asked.

"I think so. A little stressed, but I'm good."

"Is your mother okay?"

"She's fine. Why?"

"I left your suite so that you could have a private moment with her. She appeared to be in shock."

"Right. I remember now." Dammit. I forgot that. This covert activity is a tricky business.

"Well?" he asked.

"Well what?"

"Is she okay?"

"Yeah... she just got a call from her shop, Bohemian Bliss. I guess there's a... a... a dream catcher shortage. It's part of that supply chain problem. She'll be fine."

Cassie got caught up in watching Jonathan and me and paid no attention to her assigned task. I wrapped my arms around Jonathan and flipped my fingers at her a few times in a desperate signal for her to get to work. She nodded and began her search.

My armpits began sweating as Cassie rummaged for the key card without results.

"Aaaand..." I said, stretching out the word as a stall tactic while keeping Cassie in my peripheral vision.

"And what?"

"And..." My mind drew yet another blank. Watching Cassie's fruitless search while creating a conversation with Jonathan had caused a logjam in my brain. I had no idea what to say, but I know I had to keep talking to buy Cassie more time. "And... I appreciate you marrying me. It's very nice of you... to be so... nice... and patient... with the weather thing... So... it's hard to know the right words.. the right words to say... and that trip to Oxnard was... interesting. Don't ya think?" Ouch. That was so stupid. If there were a rewind button, I would have punched it several times.

He glanced back at Cassie. She froze, stopped searching, and stood up straight.

He turned back toward me. "Is that what you came here to say?"

Cassie opened a dresser drawer, then shouted, "I'm quite impressed with the sturdiness of this furniture. They didn't cut corners by furnishing these rooms with cheap stuff, that's for sure." She opened several more drawers. "Look how these drawers slide!"

I faked a chuckle. "She loves quality."

Turning my attention back to Jonathan, I said, "I'm sorry. You were saying?"

He touched my arm. "I was asking what *you* were trying to say."

"I forgot."

"Piper, you're acting very strange."

Cassie kept pretending to be impressed by the ability of furniture drawers to function without a hitch.

"I remember now," I said. "I want you to take your allergy medicine tonight, so you'll be okay tomorrow."

"No. That stuff knocks me out."

"That's okay. You'll get a good night's sleep."

"I don't want to be that drowsy. It's too strong."

"Jonathan, I insist."

"I'll go down to the store in the lobby and get that non-drowsy brand."

"That's not necessary." I hurried to his bathroom, searched for his overnight bag, and found the bottle containing his allergy medicine. I filled a glass with water and all but shoved the pill into his mouth. I handed him the glass of water. Despite his reluctance, he swallowed the medication.

"Well, don't expect anything from me till morning," he said. "I'll be out like a light."

"Got it!" said Cassie.

Jonathan spun around. "Got what?"

Her eyes darted back and forth as she thought. "Oh. I said *I got it*, didn't I? I meant *I get it*. I get why the furniture is so sturdy. The public can be rough on stuff. Let's go, Piper. It's late!"

He stared with a dumbfounded expression as I hurried to the door. I patted Cassie on the arm, and we both hurried out of his hotel room.

We dashed down the hallway to my suite, hurried inside, and shut the door.

Cassie faced my mother and held up Jonathan's key card. "Mission accomplished!"

"You did it! I'm impressed," said my mother. "I'm also going to watch you two like a hawk if you ever come over to *my* place."

Cassie nearly floated through the room on her natural high. "It was such a rush! Harmony, you should've seen me. I should be a secret agent!"

"Or a case study at a mental asylum," I said.

"You know I was good," Cassie said.

I rolled my eyes. "You were weird. Luckily, he'll be so looped by morning that he won't remember a thing."

"You drugged him?" my mother asked.

"No. I didn't drug him. I would never do that. His allergy medicine is way too strong for him, and it knocks him out, so I encouraged him to take a double dose. And in case you find yourself on a witness stand someday, I want to emphasize the word *encouraged*."

"She threw the pill down his throat and rubbed his nose," Cassie said.

My mother turned toward me. "He's not a dog, Piper."

"She exaggerates," I said. "Anyway, he'll be fine by about noon tomorrow."

I arrived at Jonathan's hotel door an hour later and swiped the key card. I opened the door an inch at a time. The room was black with no sign of life. I tiptoed through the suite's sitting room and headed for his bedroom door, where I stopped and listened again. He was snoring like a storm front passing through a wedding venue. I crept into his room. A small nightlight cast a faint light. I froze and caught my breath. My head jerked away, and I diverted my eyes to the ceiling. He lay on his stomach, his arms and legs sprawled out like a stark-naked skydiver. Any other time, I might have spent a minute or two taking in the view of his toned, tanned, and muscular body, but I was in no mood for that. After all, there's a slight chance he might be my broth—never mind. Forget I even mentioned that. Anyway, until I confirm the connection—or lack of connection—between his genealogy and mine, I'll stare at the ceiling. While still looking up, I grabbed the sheet from the foot of the bed and pulled it up past his waist.

I returned to my suite.

"The coast is clear. He's out cold," I said.

"What's the plan?" my mother asked.

"Sherman told me to swab his cheek."

Cassie said, "I'll stay here."

I reached for Cassie's hand. "We're all three going in. I need your support."

I retrieved several Q-tips from the bathroom and held them up for the other two to see. With the determination of a used car salesman on straight commission, I said, "Let's *do* this."

One by one, we slipped through his door and into the dark room.

When we reached his bedroom doorway, Cassie said, "I'll stand guard out here."

I whispered to my mother, "He was naked, but I covered him up. I hope he didn't kick the sheet off."

Cassie said, "Okay, I better go in too."

We crept to the side of the bed. Jonathan was still face down, the sheet covering him to his waist. My mother began to pull the sheet off his body, exposing the top of his butt.

I grabbed her hand and whispered, "What are you doing?"

"Helping you swab."

"Not *that* cheek."

As she pulled the sheet up to cover him, Cassie grabbed my mother's hand, stopping her.

"It's okay," Cassie whispered. "You might wake him."

I frowned at Cassie and pulled the sheet back up, covering him at least to his waist.

He slept with the side of his head on a pillow. I leaned closer to his face and tried to insert the cotton swab into his mouth. He clenched his teeth.

"I can't get it in there," I whispered.

He mumbled and rolled over, face up. We froze. I was glad I covered him. After a minute passed, I tried again to swab his cheek. He snored again. Each time he inhaled; his jaw dropped open. I timed my next move. When he inhaled, I inserted the cotton swab into his mouth, attempting to rub it against the inside of his cheek. Satisfied that I'd made sufficient contact with the cheek, I began pulling out the Q-tip. At that moment, he clenched his teeth again, leaving me staring at a Q-tip, minus the cotton tip. My eyes widened as I held the headless stick up for the others to see.

Jonathan inhaled again and choked on the cotton tip. He coughed. With his lips closed, he moved his tongue around inside his mouth. He parted his lips, exposing the cotton tip resting on the end of his tongue. He closed his mouth again and, while in a deep sleep, blew the cotton tip into the air. I tried to follow the trajectory of the cotton tip, but it disappeared in the darkness. I motioned for my mother and Cassie to follow me.

We returned to my suite.

"That's not going to work," I said. "He almost choked to death."

My mother said, "We can't give up."

I rummaged through my purse and found nail scissors.

"Sherman also told me that a sample of hair will do. Let's go back in, girls."

My mother was confused. "Hair? From where?"

"His head. Where else?"

Cassie's mouth formed into a pout.

I pursed my lips and said to Cassie, "I know what you're thinking. I don't want scissors near that area—just in case there *is* a wedding night."

A minute later, we were back in Jonathan's hotel room, tiptoeing toward his bed.

He was still asleep and, more importantly, still alive after surviving a visit from the Cotton Swab Gang.

He had rolled onto his stomach again.

I leaned over him to snip a lock of hair without touching his scalp. Every time I tried to cut a lock of hair, he moved his head and groaned.

He blinked his eyes open and squinted into the darkness. He was groggy and called out, "Piper?"

We all froze.

"Piper?"

We remained still.

"Pookie, baby, is that you?"

Cassie shot me a questioning look and mouthed *Pookie*?

I blushed and shrugged.

Jonathan rolled over until he was face up. He moaned, lifted his head slightly, and spoke again, his voice weak and slurred. "Piper? Is that you?"

I leaned closer to his ear and whispered, "You're dreaming. I'm really not here."

Jonathan's head fell back onto the bed. Then he began to talk in his sleep. His speech was garbled. Still, the words were decipherable. "Piper, baby, where did you learn that?" He giggled.

I turned back toward my mother and Cassie. I raised my palms upward and shook my head, conveying I had no idea what he was talking about.

Cassie smirked.

Jonathan continued talking in his sleep. "You're so beautiful, honey. I want to tell you something. You're the most beautiful girl I've dated—since college."

I mouthed the words *since college*? I narrowed my eyes and clenched my teeth.

My mother enjoyed that and snickered.

Jonathan continued his slurred ramblings. "C'mon, baby, let's play around. Don't be shy. Your mother is in her room and can't hear us. Besides, she could probably write a book on this stuff."

My mother made a fist and stepped toward Jonathan, but Cassie held her back.

I attempted to snip a strand of hair from his head again, but he lifted his arm each time and waved his hand over his head. "No, no, no," he slurred.

"I can't get at his head," I whispered to the others.

"Try another place," Cassie said as she lifted the sheet and peeked under it.

I wagged my finger at Cassie and lowered the sheet.

"It's okay," Cassie said. "*I'm* the only one here who can definitely say I'm not related to him." She grabbed the scissors from me and reached under the sheet.

Snip!

My mother popped open a clear sandwich bag, and Cassie dropped the hair into it like they'd done it a thousand times.

Jonathan's eyes opened, and he squinted at Cassie. His hands instinctively reached for his groin.

His jaw dropped as he stared at her.

All she could think of was, "Hi."

The three of us ran from the room and toward the door.

I glanced back as Jonathan fell out of bed. He tried to stand, tripped over his shoes, and fell face first on the floor.

CHAPTER 25

The three of us scurried back to my suite and slammed the door behind us. We took a moment to catch our breath.

"I hope he doesn't remember that in the morning," Cassie said.

My mother doubled over, hands on her knees, panting.

I pulled the scissors from my pocket. "Mother, I need a lock of your hair." I cut a few strands, trying to avoid some of the blue-streaked hair. "I won't be surprised if the DNA test results include the word *Smurf*." I placed her sample in another plastic bag.

"Shouldn't you be the one giving the sample?" Cassie asked me.

"My mother's sample will tell us everything we need to know."

My phone rang. "It's Sherman," I said, touching the screen. "Hi, Sherman."

Sherman's voice emanated from the phone's speaker. "Why aren't you answering my knock?"

"You've been knocking? We didn't hear you knock."

"Room 714, right?" he asked.

"That's the right room." I set my phone down. "Hang on."

I opened the door. Sherman was knocking on the door across the hallway.

I shook my head. "Sherman."

He stopped mid-knock and whirled around.

"That's room 711," I said. "This is 714."

Sherman squinted at the door number. "Oh."

He followed me into my hotel suite and closed the door.

My mother ran to Sherman and wrapped her arms around him. "I just love this quirky kid!"

Sherman had been called many things before: Geek, nerd, absent-minded, shy, pencil-pusher, lab rat, goofy—but *quirky* was new. And he didn't like that one either.

"Let go of him, Mother. He has work to do."

She patted him on the head as she released him.

I handed the two plastic bags containing the hair samples to Sherman.

"What's this all about? Why the big rush for test results?" Sherman asked.

I cringed. "It's a long story. I'll fill you in tomorrow when we have more time."

He squinted at the sample containing brunette and blue hair.

Cassie said, "If you're going to make a Smurf joke, somebody beat you to it."

Sherman's eyebrows raised. "What's a Smurf?"

"It was a dumb joke," I said. "Now, if you don't mind, you'd better get going. There's no time to lose." I reached out and squeezed his arm. "I owe you one, little buddy. You have no idea how important this is."

As soon as I let go, my mother stepped forward and added another hug. Cassie's goodbye gesture was a short wave of her hand.

"Hold on!" my mother said. She ran to her oversized handbag and returned to Sherman with a dream catcher.

"What's this?" Sherman asked.

"Keep it in the lab. Maybe it'll catch Piper's dreams for safekeeping."

Sherman hurried out the door and down the hall. I stood there with the door open and waited. Four seconds later, Sherman ran by my doorway again, this time in the right direction.

I closed the door and brought my hands together in a prayer-like position. Facing Cassie and my mother, I said. "In the past, I've prayed hardest when I'm nauseous or when I flush in someone else's bathroom and the toilet water is about to overflow. Today's situation tops both."

The sun rose over the mountains east of Santa Barbara. Seagulls floated in the ocean breeze while the gentle waves provided a steady rhythm to the coastal town.

Howie and the groomsmen were busy piecing together the wedding site on the sandy beach. They rebuilt the floral wedding arch, organized the chairs in rows with a sandy aisle, and created a boundary with potted flowers and lacy queen palms.

I sat slumped in a chair on the balcony of the bridal suite. My eyes were puffy and red from not sleeping. I had a serious and sober expression on my face. This was the day I'd dreamed of for so long. I was supposed to be filled with excitement, eager to start a brand-new chapter of my life with my soulmate. But it didn't feel like that at all. My stomach burned with anxiety, and a heavy weight pulled at my heart. Everything I held sacred and important hinged on a stupid DNA test. The cold, calculated outcome of an unsympathetic and uncaring lab test will determine if this magical day proceeds or stops in its tracks like a wedding limo hitting a brick wall.

Somebody knocked on the door and I moved like a snail to answer it. It was Walter and my mother. Walter was holding a large leather-bound book and plopped it down on the table. He grinned as he stepped back and dusted off his hands on his pants.

"This is the book!" he said.

I had no idea what he was talking about. "What book? I don't get it."

My mother stepped over to me, lowered her voice, and said, "I couldn't stop him. He insisted on showing you."

"Jonathan didn't tell you? C'mon! I'm sure he did," Walter said.

I shrugged.

Walter's hand landed on the book with a resounding slap. "This is our family tradition!" Walter chuckled. "For generations, every bride and groom, after the ceremony, signed their names in the brackets!"

"Why? What's the point of signing our names?" I asked.

Walter stood straight; his chest swelled with pride. "This is a Knight family tradition—our family tree! We keep it open for everyone to see on the wedding day." He turned to my mother. "Oh, and Chipmunk, since we didn't have a chance the other day, we'll fill in our names too! Right in front of everybody!" Walter walked through the sliding glass doors and onto the balcony. "It's a helluva day for a wedding!"

My mother leaned closer to me. "If Sherman doesn't get here fast with good news, we could have a lopsided tree."

"Don't say that. Don't even think those thoughts. Everything's going to be fine."

I struggled to hold back my tears.

From the balcony, Walter glanced back at us. "I *told* you the Knight family tree tradition would make her cry. Chipmunk, when you sign in, you'll cry too. You just watch."

"I might," my mother said.

Walter faced the beach again, leaned on the balcony railing, and kept an eye on the wedding site crew.

Someone else knocked at my hotel room door.

My breathing quickened. "Oh, God. That might be Sherman. This is it!"

My mother opened the door and Cassie stepped in.

My shoulders slumped as I let out a long breath.

"Gee, glad to see you too," Cassie said, shaking her head.

"Sorry. I thought it was Sherman. I'm a nervous wreck." I sat down. "The next time my client waits nervously while the jury is out, I'll understand."

"Why doesn't he just call?"

"He texted me saying he's on his way. He wants to bring me the paperwork with the test results."

"Hey, let's try your wedding dress on," Cassie said. "You know, make sure everything is alright. It'll feel better to take your mind off things."

"I can't do that yet. I mean, I know everything's okay; I just need the official results."

Another knock on the door.

My fingers dug into the arms of the chair. My heart pounded in my chest.

My mother opened the door. Sherman stood there, holding a large envelope. He tried to dodge my mother's hug, but his mousy ways were no match for her cat-like quickness. She wrapped her arms around his neck and squeezed hard. After he broke free, he straightened his shirt and collar and waved at Cassie and me.

"I got the results!" Sherman said. "Took me all night."

I tried to glean information from his words and demeanor. If he brought bad news, would he be mentioning that it took him all night to get it? Who would care at that point? So that's a good sign. On the other hand, if it were good news, why wouldn't he announce it right away? I didn't know what to think.

I rose from the chair, trembling. My legs wobbled, and I nearly tipped over. Cassie ran to my side and propped me up.

"Mother, come here. I need you too. Hold on to me."

My mother stepped to my side. She brushed my hair from my face and said, "It's alright, sweetie. It's going to be fine. I'm here."

"Okay, Sherman. We're out of time. What's the verdict? Jonathan and my mother aren't related, right?" I asked, swallowing hard and shaking like a leaf.

Sherman said, "Well, the DNA results show—" His eyes darted toward the table. "Are those wedding cake poppers?"

"Sherman!" we all shouted.

"Sorry, I just love those." He pulled the paperwork out of the envelope and reviewed several pages.

"You can't remember the results?" Cassie asked.

"I just want to make sure I'm right." His eyes stopped at a particular line in the report. "Oh, yeah. That's right. The results. There they are."

I held on to Cassie and my mother.

Sherman continued. "The results show that you and Jonathan

are—" He moved the paperwork closer to his eyes.

"Go on," I said.

"Okay. You and Jonathan are definitely… siblings."

My legs buckled. I gasped for breath, but the room didn't seem to have enough oxygen.

"Breathe, sweetie," my mother said.

Cassie tried to lift me to my feet. "Sherman, get a glass of water."

"I'm fine, thank you," he said.

"Not for you! For Piper!" Cassie shouted.

Cassie helped me to the sofa.

I was hysterical and tried to catch my breath. While crying, I said, "My wedding! My marriage! Everything is ruined!" I put my hand on my chest. "My angina."

My mother said, "There'll be no wedding night, sweetie. No need to worry about *that* part of your body."

"My *heart*, mother. My heart is literally broken."

Sherman returned with a glass of water, but I waved him off.

"I can't face Jonathan," I said, my watery eyes moving from my mother to Cassie. "How do I tell him something I refuse to believe myself?"

"The accuracy rate, as a percentage," Sherman said, "is ninety-nine point nine, nine, nine—"

"Sherman!" Cassie said, shaking her head.

Walter left the balcony and walked into the suite. He glanced at me as I cried on the sofa with my hand on my chest. "What the hell is going on here? Is it her angina?"

My mother shook her head. "Men, with their one-track minds."

Cassie stooped next to me and whispered into my ear. "We should call Jonathan."

I cried harder and buried my face in my hands.

Cassie dialed Jonathan's number. "This is Cassie… will you please come to Piper's room?… I know it's bad luck on the wedding day. Don't worry about that now… Okay."

A few minutes later, Jonathan entered my suite. I was

slumped over in a chair and crying. My mother was consoling me. Jonathan tried to rush to me, but Cassie stood in his way.

"Cassie, would you please move? I need to be with Piper."

She wouldn't let him pass.

I stopped sobbing just enough to say, "No, Jonathan. Stay there. This isn't going to be easy." I wobbled to my feet with my mother's help. "Jonathan, it's the worst possible news. I don't even know how to tell you."

"What could be so bad? We've overcome a lot, and we'll overcome whatever this is about. Just talk to me. We've got a wedding to get to."

My mother said, "Wally, you better sit down, too."

Cassie picked up a box of tissues and brought it to me.

I pulled several tissues out of the box and dabbed my eyes. "I don't know where to start."

"Just talk to me," Jonathan said.

I wiped my nose. My throat was tight with emotion, and I barely got the words out. "First of all, I want you to know that what I'm about to tell you is something that, in my heart, I'll never ever believe—regardless of what the results say."

"Results?"

I nodded. "Until the day I die, I'll be in denial about this. But sometimes, life takes twists and turns no one can explain. Life is cruel and unfair, and this is totally unfair."

"Please. Just say it."

I continued to sob and pulled several more tissues out of the box. "Thirty years ago, a baby boy was given up for adoption in New York City. The birth mother did not want to meet the adoptive parents. She even went on to have a baby girl two years later. This is where it gets hard to say. That baby girl she had two years later... That was me."

"Okay. Fine. What's the problem? So your mother gave the boy up for adoption. Depending on the circumstance, that can be a noble thing to do."

I braced myself. "The baby boy she gave up two years earlier? They tell me... that was you."

My words caused Jonathan to stagger backward. "No. No way. I don't believe this."

Tears streamed down my cheeks. "I know. I don't either."

"If I'm that baby boy, then you're saying Harmony is my mother? That makes you my... my... No! I refuse to believe this! I won't!" He pointed to my mother. "This is not my mother!" He glanced at Walter. "Dad. Say something!"

Walter's eyes widened. His hand clutched his chest, and his breathing quickened. "This is preposterous!"

"Clear it up, Dad. Tell them they're wrong!"

Walter said, "I never met the birth mother. I have no way to prove this story is false."

Sherman held up his index finger, turned to Jonathan, and said, "I'm pretty sure you're her son. I did a DNA test. Do you want to hear the accuracy percentage?"

"We don't need to hear the numbers again," Cassie said.

"I still have the DNA samples at the lab, if anyone wants to verify them."

Jonathan shook his head. "You couldn't have taken a test. To do that, you'd need a sample from me! And I never gave anyone a DNA sample or a strand of hair—" Then he paused. "Weird. I had a dream last night that—"

Cassie cringed and raised her hand. "That was me. Collecting your sample. Sorry."

Jonathan took one step toward me. "This is not true. There's no way. I don't need a lab result to tell me something I already know. We're not related. I know it in my heart."

I leaned my head to one side. "That's how *I* feel."

"This is crazy," Jonathan shouted. "There's been a mistake. We'll take another DNA test to prove it."

"I ran the test twice," Sherman said.

Jonathan threw his hands up in frustration. "I don't know how to handle this."

I stopped crying long enough to say, "I'm so sorry."

Jonathan moved backward toward the door, one small step at a time. His eyes pointed at the floor. "I—I've got to go. I just need to go."

    He opened the door, and without another word, walked out of my life.

CHAPTER 26

By the next morning, the floral wedding arch had drifted away with the tide, along with my lifelong dream of being married.

I slumped over the rail of the bridal suite balcony, staring down at the abandoned wedding site.

Howie and the groomsmen were stacking the white folding chairs, and Brother Larry sat cross-legged on the sand where the altar would have been. His chin rested on his fist while he drew endless circles in the sand with a piece of driftwood. The seagulls still sailed overhead in the wind, but they lacked the cheerfulness they exhibited the previous day.

Directly below, near the hotel doors, a rambunctious crowd milled about.

Watching the dismantling of the wedding venue was too much to handle, so I stepped through the sliding glass door and went inside.

My mother and Walter were at the kitchen table sipping coffee. My appearance provided plenty of ammunition for snide comments, but they were merciful and didn't say a word. They continued sipping coffee and focused on each other, pretending not to notice my messy hair mashed flat on one side, tissues overflowing from my bathrobe pockets, and my streaked mascara. Nor did they say one word about the long strand of toilet paper stuck to the heel of my fuzzy pink slippers. The only upside to my ghastly appearance was the red in my bloodshot eyes, which provided a hint of color to my otherwise pale face.

Surely, my sobbing kept them up most of the night, as evidenced by their tired but sympathetic eyes.

My mother forced a smile. "Good morning, sweetie."

"There's nothing good about it," I muttered. "I'm glad we're all checking out of this damn hotel this morning. I never want to see it again in my life."

Walter said, "I'm sorry for the way it all ended yesterday. I wish I could make everything okay."

"Time heals all," my mother said.

"Time won't help this," I said. "Nothing will."

The sound of people talking and shouting rose from the street.

"Who are those people near the hotel?" I asked.

Walter shook his head. "Somehow, Malcolm Hyde discovered the reason behind the wedding cancelation. That racket down below is the media camped out on the sidewalk. Bunch of vultures! Unless there's a miracle, Jonathan's campaign will definitely come to an end. Poor boy."

My mother said, "We assume they're outside Jonathan's house too, but Wally hasn't been able to reach him. Have you heard from him?"

"Let him go, Mother. Just let him go. He's as lost as I am."

"Yesterday, he was dressing for the wedding and had me hold his wallet and phone for him," Walter said. "I still have his ATM card and everything else. He can't go far without those things."

Someone knocked on the door. My mother opened it to find Sherman standing in the hall.

"Hi, sweetie," she said to Sherman.

"Is Piper here?"

"She is. Come in."

My mother held Sherman's arm and walked him toward the kitchen.

"Did you see all the reporters on the street?" Sherman asked.

"We're still trying to figure out how they found out so quickly about…" Walter didn't finish his sentence.

Sherman shrugged his shoulders. "There was only one guy out there yesterday. Now there's a hundred."

"One guy?" Walter asked.

"It was that guy in the blue Dodger cap. I apologized for breaking his camera the other night. He forgave me. We talked for quite a while. Nice guy."

Walter raised one eyebrow. "Did you talk to your new friend in the cap *after* the DNA results?"

Sherman paused a moment, then said, "Yeah, I think I did."

Walter lowered his voice and said to my mother, "The race for the biggest doofus was Howie's to win, but Sherman just took the lead."

Sherman handed me an envelope. "This is for you."

"What now? I can't take any more bad news."

As I grabbed it from him, he said, "The venue manager at the beach gave it to me. I assumed it was an invoice when I read *Piper's Venue*."

"Sherman, it says *Parking Violation*."

"No, it doesn't. It says *Piper's Venue*. Let me see it again." He took the envelope and read it out loud. *Piper's Venue.* See?"

He tried to hand the envelope back to me, but I pushed it back at him.

"Sherman, read it again." He squinted at the envelope. "*Piper's Ven*—wait. *Parking Venue*."

"Seriously, Sherman? You can't read that?" I pointed to the words.

Sherman tried again. "*Parking Venue*. Wait. *Parking Violation*." His eyes lifted to meet mine. "Oh."

I grabbed his arm and pulled him behind me as I marched toward my suite's front door.

"Don't hurt that boy!" my mother shouted. She turned to Walter. "I feel sorry for him. Is that weird?"

"Very," Walter said.

Sherman and I were gone for about twenty minutes before I brought him back to my bridal suite. I opened the door and pulled him inside.

Jonathan was there.

I stopped walking and froze. Sherman ran into the back of me.

"Jonathan just got here," my mother said to me.

Jonathan stared at the floor while he spoke to me. "I left my wallet and phone. I was just leaving."

Walter asked, "Son, how'd you get through that mob of reporters? Did they bother you?"

"I don't care what they think anymore."

My mother rose from the table and stood next to Walter. "I'm so sorry, Jonathan. It's all my fault. I've ruined your life and Piper's, too."

Walter turned and said, "Chipmunk, it's not your fault. You had no idea these kids would eventually meet on the other side of the country. Don't be hard on yourself."

"Dad? The wallet and phone? I need to go. This is not where I want to be."

I pulled Sherman closer to where Jonathan stood. "Jonathan, I'm glad you're here."

Jonathan said, "Please, I can't take any more—"

"Sorry, but you need to hear this. First of all, the good news is, Sherman's blind as a bat."

"That's not good news, sweetie," my mother said.

"But the truth is, he can hardly read a thing. Not even an envelope that's clearly labeled *parking violation*."

"Okay, I'm sorry to hear that," Jonathan said, "but I don't have time for this. I just want to go."

I took one step closer to Jonathan and said, "I'm sorry for collecting your DNA sample without your permission, but my mother was telling crazy stories about her wild life, and we let our imaginations get carried away. After that, I had to find out if what I feared most was true."

"It doesn't matter anymore," Jonathan said, his head still hanging low.

I pulled up a chair and forced Sherman to sit down. "Sherman and I just reviewed the lab paperwork he still had in his room." I turned to Sherman. "Raise your right hand."

"What?"

"Just do it. Raise your right hand." I raised mine as an example.

He partially raised his right hand.

"Sherman, do you promise to tell the truth, the whole truth, and nothing but the truth?"

"Of course."

He lowered his hand.

I paced in front of Sherman. "In your analysis of the DNA results, did you base your conclusions on what you read?"

"Uh, yeah."

"Did anyone assist you in your analysis?"

"No. Wait. Yes, just now. *You* did, Piper."

"And in our review of your work, did we determine that, indeed, you are legally blind as a bat?"

My mother said to Walter, "She's badgering the witness."

Walter asked, "Can we stop this nonsense and have a normal conversation?"

"Objection!" I said, pointing to Walter. "If I may, I'd like to proceed."

"Objection sustained, Dad," Jonathan said.

I turned away from Sherman. "I need to have a sidebar." I stepped over to Jonathan, lowered my voice, and asked, "Are you paying attention?"

His lips curled up a bit at the corners. "Maybe."

I turned back to the witness—I mean, Sherman. "Did you get everything screwed up, as usual?"

Sherman glanced at my mother for help.

I leaned toward him. "Answer the question, Sherman. Did you read the results wrong? Yes or no?"

"I guess so."

I stopped and stared into Sherman's eyes. "As my so-called expert witness, answer this. Does Jonathan's DNA match anyone in this room?"

I spun around and faced my mother, Walter, and Jonathan.

Sherman sighed. "There was a DNA match, but did Jonathan's DNA match anyone here?" He paused. "No."

I stepped over to Jonathan. My voice strained with emotion and my eyes filled with tears. "So now that we know the truth, I want to ask you this. Jonathan Knight, will you marry me?" I took a step back. "I'll wait for the verdict."

Jonathan turned to Walter and my mother, then back to me. "I sentence you, Piper, to life in matrimony—with me."

I burst into tears—tears of joy. Jonathan threw his arms around me, lifted me off the ground, and turned in slow circles as we kissed. He lowered my feet to the floor and wiped the tears from my face.

My mother clapped while Walter wrapped his arm around her.

I said to Jonathan, "In my heart, I never doubted, not for one second, that you were anything other than the one fate meant for me."

"I'm right with you on that. You are, and always will be, the love of my life."

"I do have one question," I said. "At our wedding, is it okay if Tanya comes?"

We all laughed.

"You can invite *all* your goofy relatives. The more, the merrier."

My mother shook her finger at Jonathan as we all chuckled again. Then her eyes widened. "Wait! Wait! Hold on!" she said. "If *Jonathan's* DNA didn't match anyone in this room—who was the match?"

Sherman's eyebrows raised as he glanced at me.

"Go ahead," I said to him.

Sherman cleared his throat. "Well, as Piper said, I misread the names on the samples." He turned to my mother. "I was working on my own DNA sample and set mine next to yours and Jonathan's. Then I confused my sample with his."

My mother tilted her head. "I don't get it. So, whose DNA matched?"

Sherman's face reddened. "I'll answer it this way." He took a step closer to my mother. "Can I call you... *Mom*?"

My mother screamed with delight and jumped up and down.

"I knew it! My baby boy is back! He's come back to me!" She placed both arms around him and squeezed him tight, kissing his forehead a hundred times. "I could sense the connection all along!"

I shook my head in amazement.

Walter asked my mother, "He won't be living with us, will he?"

My mother grinned. "For as long as he wants!"

I turned to Jonathan. "So, my brother turns out to be Sherman. Things just keep getting weirder."

Jonathan pressed his lips against mine. "I missed kissing you. I couldn't for two days, and it almost killed me." He kissed me again.

"Don't ever stop," I said.

"Come here," he said. He took my hand in his and pulled me to the window. He opened the drapes. "Let's give 'em something to talk about."

As he moved closer, I placed my fingers on his approaching lips. "Wait. The reporters—they can see us. You don't care?"

After peering at the street below, he shrugged and gazed into my eyes. "I couldn't care less. We have nothing to hide." He parted his lips and placed his mouth on mine as the cameras below flashed wildly.

CHAPTER 27

Later that afternoon, on the beach, Brother Larry wiped the sweat from his forehead. "At this moment, I pronounce you husband and wife. You may now kiss the bride."

My mother clapped and wiped a tear while Walter rolled his eyes.

Brother Larry smiled at Cassie and Howie. Howie leaned forward and kissed his bride, Cassie.

Cassie pumped her fist in the air with one hand and, with the other, raised her bouquet in the air. "Whoo-hoo!"

I stood at Cassie's side as her maid of honor, and Jonathan was on the other side of Howie, serving as Howie's best man. Jonathan and I leaned back to see each other. I smiled at him, and he winked back at me.

Cassie turned to me with a sparkle in her eyes. "Only a cheapskate like Howie would take advantage of this opportunity to get married for free. He's such a doofus—but he's *my* doofus."

Cassie and Howie strode hand in hand down the aisle between the mostly empty white folding chairs.

Jonathan stepped forward and held his elbow out. I threaded my arm through his, and we followed the newlyweds.

"Can you believe they got married?" I asked.

"Like Howie said, 'Why not? Brother Larry was sitting around with nothing to do.'" As we walked, Jonathan turned to me. "You okay? This was supposed to be your big day."

"This is *their* day. Ours will come soon enough." I smiled.

"That's quite a statement, coming from someone whose entire focus was the wedding ceremony."

I was as relaxed and happy as I'd ever been. "As long as you're by my side, that's all that matters."

"So, no regrets? Our love-at-first-sight relationship was not a mistake?"

I took a moment to consider my answer. "At first, in my naïve way of thinking, I used to think that falling for someone so quickly and completely was all that mattered. I told myself that as long as there was true love, all the other pieces would fall into place. It turns out… I was right."

When we reached the end of the aisle, Jonathan exhaled, grimaced, and said, "The sand is hot. Can I put my shoes back on now?"

"Yes, you can."

ABOUT THE AUTHOR

Kammie C. Rose

Thank you for reading The Problem With Love at First Sight.
I hope you enjoyed the story. I had so much fun writing it.
Authors depend on reviews to help their books find success. I would appreciate it so much if you'd take the time to rate or review this book on Amazon.
Thank you!
Drop me an email at kammieCrose@outlook.com
I'd love to hear from you!

BOOKS BY THIS AUTHOR

The Problem With Time Travel

Brian is in the marriage from hell. He is given the chance to travel back in time to his high school reunion and undo the terrible choice he made when he chose the evil Gwyneth over the love of his life, Meggie.
Brian learns that tempting fate is a tricky business and his missteps create a chain reaction of catastrophes he must correct. How to deal with running into himself was not in the time travel instruction booklet.
Meggie's life hangs in the balance.

The Big Rewrite

Olivia, a struggling songwriter, is pressured by her Nashville publisher to co-write with the man she despises--mega star Luke Travis. She wants to keep it strictly business, but Luke pursues her romantically. To complicate things, Luke is holding back a secret that could change everything.

My What-If Girl

A friends to lovers story. Everyone carries a flame for that one person they can't quite get over. The one that makes you wonder what if... What if I had only said this, or what if I'd only done that, would we be together?
Annika tries to keep her feelings for Baker private while she helps him pursue his what-if girl, Sienna, a Hollywood celebrity.

Made in the USA
Columbia, SC
30 January 2024